Worth
The *Fall*

Bonnie
my favorite NYC
Ray of Sunshine!
KK,
Bria Q

Bria Quinlan

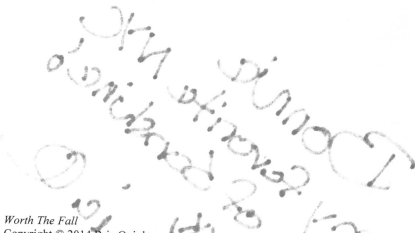

Worth The Fall
Copyright © 2014 Bria Quinlan
All rights reserved.

BREW HA HA SERIES

It's in His Kiss
The Last Single Girl
Worth the Fall
The Catching Kind

BREW AFTER DARK Shorts
Love in Tune
Sweet As Cake

~*~

YA Books by Bria Quinlan

Secret Girlfriend (RVHS #1)
Secret Life (RVHS #2)
Wreckless

ONE

Y OU'RE DUMPING ME?"
I could *not* believe this was happening. Every
time. Every time I thought this week couldn't get
worse—BAM! It did.

"Come on, Kasey. You can't be shocked by this." Jason
looked at me over the very nice, very expensive dinner he'd
invited me to, pity shining through those narrowed eyes.

I sucked in a deep breath, glancing away to focus because
this just didn't make sense.

"You're really doing this tonight? Seriously?" At the
moment, I was more shocked than heartbroken. Although, as
I pondered it, heartbreak would probably attack as soon as I
was home alone in my apartment...my very, *very* empty
apartment.

I'd have to sit on the floor to have a good cry.

"I'm sorry you're so surprised," Jason said, although he
didn't sound the least bit sorry.

"Surprised? I was supposed to move in with you this weekend."

He tipped his head to the side and looked at me like he might be humoring a child. "You can't really move in now, right?"

"Well, not if you're breaking up with me I can't, can I?" My voice shot up. It sounded a bit hysterical even to my own ears. In the back of my mind, I realized people were beginning to look our way. Jason was going to hate that.

He reached across the table and wrapped his hand around mine, giving it a harsh squeeze. Even his fake comfort was…well, fake.

"If you moved, how were you going to pay your half of the rent? How would you be able to carry your weight?"

Carry my weight? We'd been dating for almost three years and now he was dumping me because I might not be able to pay rent for a couple months on a condo he already owned?

"Give me a break, Jason. I lost my freaking job yesterday. Do you think I have nothing in the bank? You pick the day after I got laid-off to do this?" The hysteria was gone. In its place my emotional cup was filled to the brim with near-blinding rage.

"The economy is tight." He shrugged as if none of this really mattered. "Who's to say you'll find something right away?"

I could not believe this. Could. Not. Believe it. Just last week we'd finished selling all my furniture on Craigslist because his already "fit" in his place. I'd canceled my lease, paid the fine to break it, and was homeless as of the end of the month—which conveniently happened in two days.

"Here." He handed me a card.

A card. I looked at the lavender sealed envelope. Was I supposed to open it? Did Hallmark really make an I'm-Dumping-Your-Ass-But-Good-Luck-With-Everything card?

"What's this?"

"That's the first month's rent and half of the security you'd paid. I figured it was only fair to give it back."

You think? I looked down at the card again, wondering what he'd written in it, tempted to open it right then. In retrospect, giving him the security deposit should have been the first sign.

Okay, maybe not the first.

"So, where exactly do you think I'm going to live?"

Scorn. I'd moved from rage to scorn. I was now officially a woman scorned.

No wonder men weren't supposed to cross us. If hell had no fury like me at that moment, it still had a lot of leash to run on. I could have gutted him with the fancy fish knife resting against my plate.

"Well, I don't want to sound heartless," Jason continued studying his plate before looking up with the least empathetic expression I'd ever seen, "but that's not really my problem now, is it?"

The woman at the next table gasped and that's when I realized most of the tables had fallen silent to the melodrama playing out that was my life.

"No. I guess not. I guess when you dump your girlfriend because she lost her job, you think just about nothing is your problem." I pushed my chair out, wrapped myself in my Ann Taylor jacket, and picked up my purse. "Oh, wait. You know what your problem is?"

He shook his head, a small smirk yanking his mouth up into cruel tips on each side.

"Getting Bordeaux out of cashmere." I picked up our half empty bottle of wine and dumped it out on his head. "Good luck with that."

I stormed away, a smattering of applause following me in my wake. Angry tears nearly blinded me by the time I reached the lobby.

"Please. Allow me." The host pushed the door open and held it for me as I marched into the cool, spring night. "Good luck, miss."

Yeah. I was going to need it.

TWO

I N FRONT OF THE restaurant, off to the side, sat Jason's BMW M5. Just sat there. Innocently enough. Of course, it wasn't offering me a ride home and Jason had picked a restaurant nowhere near a bus or train.

But, there it was. Right there. Jason didn't believe in paying for valet parking and this spot had been dumb luck.

I waited a moment to see if he'd come out to check on me. If maybe—just maybe—he was human enough to make sure I was okay and give me a ride home.

When two minutes went by with me adjusting to the slight sting of night air, I realized there was no way he was going to waste a perfectly good steak. He'd probably stripped off that sweater, tossed it at a waitress to soak, and dug back in.

I eyed the BMW.

I eyed the valet.

I eyed the BMW again.

To be fair, it hadn't done anything to me. But, as an extension of Jason, this mess of a night, and everything that was wrong in my life right now, it was a pretty good target. Slipping down next to the front tire, I took the cap off the air valve. With my key, I slooooooowwwllly let the air out of the tire with a gentle *shush* until the rim rested on the ground.

Then I moved on to the next tire. And the next.

I considered leaving one tire inflated just because it looked out of place. But when you got right down to it, that little hiss of air was extremely cathartic. So, I deflated that one too.

Settling on a sidewalk bench, I called a cab hoping I wouldn't have cause to stress about the expense later. I ignored the chilly end-of-summer night air and waited.

It took Jason seven more minutes to finally appear. I wondered if he'd had dessert. Probably. Probably even made sure it was that flan I loved, just out of spite.

He pretended not to notice me and he definitely didn't notice all the flat tires. Until he opened the door. Then he noticed the car seemed to be a little lower than normal. Then the tires. Then me.

The look on his face—it was a beautiful thing.

He didn't approach me or come around the Beemer. He just screeched at me over the hood.

"You slashed my tires?"

"No. I would never slash anyone's tires. Even yours." Then, because I could admit to myself this might have gotten a little ridiculous—no matter how cathartic it was—I added, "Grow up."

Kettle, pot. Good times.

"So they magically flattened themselves?" Snide. How had I never noticed this snide streak in him?

Three years of not noticing? That seemed excessive even for someone as focused on her schooling and career as I had been. I began to question every conversation where he made himself out to be the clever one, smarter than everyone around him and realized clever probably hadn't been the right word. That was definitely on me. I had better get a little more aware if I was going to survive in the world as an adult.

And maybe stop insisting that Jell-O was a food group. But, some standards remained with us past childhood.

"I don't know about magic. I mean, what is magic anyway? I think it would have been magic if my cab had gotten here before you decided to see if I'd been picked up hitchhiking. But, alas, I'm still waiting." I smiled at him. One of those big, shiny smiles that really says *Ha Ha To You Buddy* instead of *Hey, You're Kinda Cute*. No more *Cute* smiles for him. "So, I suspect, the world of magic is dead."

I picked up a newspaper someone had left on the bench and pretended to read. It must have looked silly there in the dim light of the streetlamp, but it seemed like a logical prop for this farce I was finally taking an active role in.

"You think you can just flatten my tires and I'm not going to call the cops?" He was already dialing. "Hello? 911? Yeah, I want to report an assault. No. I'm not hurt. I wasn't the one assaulted."

At this point I was having a hard time believing he'd called 911—that he was calling this an assault—not to mention I'd actually dated this idiot for thirty-three months. That was more than a month for every year of my life.

Maybe *I* was the idiot.

"No," he continued, still glaring at me over the hood. "No one is hurt. Well, not hurt exactly…I'm not sure what the weapon was…No, I don't need an ambulance. Just a cop."

By this point, the host had come out to join the valet. The two whispered and stared. I heard a snicker escape from one of them.

"My car...She assaulted my car...Well, the tires are flat...Does it matter? I want a cop and I want one now."

Christmas came the same time every year. Maybe, just for the heck of it, I'd send him a copy of *How to Win Friends and Influence People*. You know, with a nice little note in the front about his people skills and a good luck with life note.

"Fine. But he better hurry. What do I do if she tries to leave?" He looked my way again, laying his hand on the hood and petting the paint job lightly. "What do you mean I can't hold her against her will? Fine. But I better hear sirens within the next three minutes."

He hung up, shoved his phone in his pocket, and he stabbed a finger at me from twelve feet away. "Do not go anywhere."

For the first time since I'd called the cabbie, I was kind of hoping he'd gotten lost. It might be worth having a record to watch Jason's tantrum play out.

When the cop showed up a few minutes later, there was a distinct lack of sirens. I was almost disappointed.

The officer got out of the car and glanced at the BMW. He shook his head a little as he reached back in the car for a notebook, straightened his cap, and then headed toward Jason.

"What seems to be the problem here, sir?"

Oh. I liked this guy already. If the flat tone of his voice showed how he was really feeling about this situation, I *really* liked him. I didn't think I was going to mind being arrested by someone who saw the ridiculousness here.

"My car has been assaulted."

I really couldn't believe he hadn't rethought that wording since hanging up with the 911 dispatcher.

"She," he stabbed that finger my way again, "attacked it."

I was back to pretending to read the newspaper and ignoring him.

"She attacked your car?" The cop was walking around the car for the second time and squatted to look at the front tire closest to the restaurant's lights. "These aren't slashed."

"They're flat." Jason sounded as if this was the equivalent of a mass war crime.

"But they aren't slashed. Someone just let the air out."

"But, they're flat." Jason finally came around the hood and kept coming. Before I knew what he was going to do, he grabbed my arm and yanked me to my feet. "She flattened my tires. I want her arrested."

How had I ever dated such an ass? Really? I should probably see a therapist just to figure out if I was over whatever stupidity I'd been living under for the last few years.

Of course, to see a therapist, I was going to need health benefits.

"Let go of me." I tried to tug my arm away, but he just gripped me tighter, his fingers biting into my skin through the light wool of my jacket. "Seriously. Let me go."

"Sir, I'm going to have to ask you to let her go."

Now the cop who had raised an eyebrow at my newspaper was coming toward us.

"Ma'am, did you see anyone flatten this guy's tires?"

"Well, I haven't been out here very long."

"About how long?" he asked.

"Well, my boyfriend—I mean, ex-boyfriend—drove me all the way out here to the middle of nowhere—"

"The middle of nowhere?" Jason couldn't even let me finish a sentence. "We're five blocks from The Village."

"Anywhere without a train is the middle of nowhere." I'd learned that lesson the hard way looking for my first apartment here.

"I was *trying* to give you one last nice meal."

"You were—"

"Ma'am. How long?" Now he was giving me the flat tone and unreadable look.

"My *ex*-boyfriend dumped me because I lost my job. He said I'd just be dead weight. After that, I came out here to wait for a cab. So, about as long as it takes a cab to get here."

The cop was smirking. Not so much that you'd notice. Just a little bit. Maybe I was imagining it, but I didn't think so. I really was going to like him. I wondered if they'd fingerprint me. Did that stuff come off with soap? I hoped it wouldn't affect my unemployment claim.

"So, not very long then?" Officer Inscrutable asked.

"I don't think so."

"You aren't buying this, are you?" Jason shook me, rattling my teeth a little.

"Sir, let her go before I toss you in the back of my car."

"But she assaulted my car."

"You can't assault a car. But you can assault a woman. If you don't let her go, I'm bringing you downtown and having your car towed. On its rims."

I may actually be in love. This whole situation was my rebound boyfriend.

Which was great because I was staying far, *far* away from guys for quite a while.

Jason's hand fell away. I doubted it had anything to do with not assaulting me and more to do with wanting the attention back on his car.

Once he let go, the officer called the valet and host over.

"Did either of you see anything happen to this car?"

Both of them shook their heads.

"Nothing? No one came and let all the air out of the tires?"

Again with the head-shaking.

"Oh, come on." Jason paced between me and the car, probably afraid I was going to make a dive at his baby again. "It's obvious these two idiots are lying."

The valet looked our way and then back at the cop. "I've been running cars since six. Someone *might* have been able to do this while I was around back." He glanced at Jason. "It really is a shame you didn't want to pay the five bucks to have your car parked."

Yeah, we could all hear the sorrow in his voice.

By this point, people were standing in the window watching. The officer had taken his little hat off and was rubbing the dark, close cut hair at the back of his head.

"So, we have no damage and no witnesses. I suspect you're just going to have to contact AAA and call it a night."

"You're not going to arrest her?" Jason sounded so shocked I almost felt bad for him.

It was kind of nice something wasn't going his way tonight. I mean, besides those four magically flattened tires.

"On what? Having dated an idiot? Sorry, but there's no law against that." The officer put his hat back on and headed toward the car. "If I get called out here again, I'm going to have you arrested for filing a false complaint. No matter what the reason is. You better hope the restaurant isn't robbed."

Jason stared after him, his jaw a bit slack at the whole lack of getting-his-own-way'ness in the situation.

I was trying not to gloat over my tiny victory. And then— in my first stroke of luck all night—as the officer walked toward his car, my ride pulled up.

"Hey." The officer called, pointing at me before ducking into his vehicle. I could see his dimple peek out from where I stood. "You. Behave."

Right. Because my plan had been mass chaos when I'd headed out this evening. I jumped in the cab before Jason could grab me again.

"Where to, miss?"

Collapsing back in the seat, I locked the door and said, "Home."

Or what was going to pass for home for two more days.

THREE

I GAVE THE CAB driver my address before I realized I hadn't been to an ATM in days. I had a bad feeling about what I was going to find in my purse. I mean, no matter how long you'd been dating someone, when he asks you out to a fancy restaurant the day before you're supposed to move in with him, you think *Am I getting jewelry*, not *Will I need cab fare*.

$1.78

How had I managed to get one of the few remaining independent cabs with no card swipe? Not good. But, luckily I'm paranoid. There's always a twenty tucked in one of the little inside pockets of my bag.

"How close to that address can I get for twenty dollars?"

The cabbie gave a deep, long-suffering sigh as if he wouldn't just be driving someone else around for the same twenty-dollar-amount-of-time if I wasn't there.

"Fine."

Fine wasn't exactly a location.

"I'm having a tough night." I gave him a big smile in the rearview mirror. But not too big. Like I'm-putting-on-a-brave-face big. Which I kind of was. Hopefully, he'd take pity on me and maybe let that twenty get me a tad further than the meter dictated.

When Jason had first let me know he was dumping me, I'd assumed there was someone else. That he'd gotten tired of me. I had already been justifying how it might have been my own fault.

I'd moved here for grad school and met him right away. He'd been one of my advisor's former TAs my final semester and was still teaching one of the segments one evening a week. He'd taken me under his wing immediately, shaping my education and career path. My time was filled with studying and him. My *friends* category was still filled by my girlfriends back home and from undergrad.

Then my internship turned into an assistant project manager position. When my boss managed to get us almost blacklisted with a client, I was pushed into a management position. I'd had to work my butt off to prove the chance they'd taken on me was worth it. That *I* was worth it.

And I loved it. I loved the drive and the hours and the push to make the best marketing campaign out there. I'd been surprised to discover most of my peers liked to do the pitching and design, but not the technical part of the creating. Or they'd like the directed creation, but not the customer work.

I adored every aspect—soup to nuts. And, so, as I worked my way past bored associates who liked to keep things status quo, I let everything else fall to the side.

I had my girls at home. I had Jason. I had a job I adored.

What else could I have needed?

I almost wish Jason *had* been cheating. At least then I could have said someone else pulled his attention away. That love had won out...or something. He'd still be a huge jerk, but at least I'd know there was a reason. Not just that I mattered so little that a potential few months' rent was a valid reason to jump ship.

I leaned my head back and watched the lights go by the window, slipping past me with a quick, silent pattern of darkness and light...darkness and light...It seemed to say, *You're an idiot...You're an idiot.*

It was sinking in. The whole he-dumped-me thing. Okay, not the dumped part. I'd caught on to that pretty quickly. More the part about how easy it was for him to drop me. How I'd been building this little dream in my head and he had just been looking for a roommate who conveniently paid half the mortgage and shared his bed.

Good luck with that on Craigslist, pal.

I had never felt so expendable in my life. My boss had even used the word. "Kasey, we have to cut some corners and while you do great work, unfortunately, you're expendable."

I'd asked what that meant. What did it mean to have three projects under your leadership, six people reporting to you, several deadlines coming up in the next two months, and still be expendable? Apparently, when you hire and train great minds right out of their undergrad program who can finish the work—even if they couldn't have gotten the contract in the first place or managed it once they had it—you're expendable. Especially if each of them only made eighty-percent of the salary you did.

Good thing I didn't have a dog. It probably would have peed *expendable* into my rug and then taken off with some hot poodle down the street while I was out.

The cab pulled to the side of the road under one of the beautiful, old oak trees lining a wide cobblestone sidewalk. My block? Regular streetlights and uneven pavement walkways. No trees.

Obviously this was not my block.

"Okay." The cabbie turned around and put his hand out.

I glanced from the flashing red meter to him. "Eighteen dollars?" Not only was he not going to drive me the extra mile home, he wasn't even going to drive me all the way to my twenty dollars.

I guess I was not one of those women who relied on the kindness of strangers.

"That's including tip."

For real? This guy was a prince. He was making Jason look decent. I was seriously considering more car assault.

I handed him the twenty and waited.

He waited.

I waited.

"Are you going to get out?"

We could have been the last mile by now.

I stuck my hand out. "Who said anything about tipping you?"

We continued our stare down until he slapped two dollars in my hand. I'd planned on giving him the one-seventy-eight in my wallet as a tip, but he'd just ticked me off.

On the upside, I now had three-seventy-eight. Yeah, that was going to save the day.

I shoved the door open and slid my legs out as gracefully as I could in a tiny skirt and ridiculously high Special Occasion Heels. I straightened and found myself deserted in front of a coffee shop in a quaint neighborhood I could never afford. It had those little lamps that looked like gaslights from back in the Jack the Ripper days and charming green shutters around black-framed windows. The door was a heavy, oak thing that made me think I was on the edge of a little Irish village. Look at me, I know charming when I see it.

A gold-on-maroon sign over the door announced I'd arrived at the Brew Ha Ha.

Well, that pretty much summed up my night in a sad, punny kind of way. Plus, caffeine seemed like a good idea before my stiletto'd walk home.

Glancing at my shoes, I couldn't help but wonder what I'd been thinking when I'd bought them. I mean, they were expensive, not my style, and amazingly uncomfortable. But the woman had said my boyfriend would love them. I, being the idiot I just discovered I was, bought them.

And now, I was paying the price. Figuratively and literally.

I pushed the door open and sucked in a cleansing breath of coffee scented air. The comfort and warmth eased up my skin, gentling every nerve that had been on high alert since the night had turned down that unexpected lane of singleness. There were collections of overstuffed chairs with coffee tables and straight back seats around scruffy wooden tables. A "Gently Read" sign rested against a bookshelf in the corner with a collection of used books. It even had a fireplace against the far wall with the sooty evidence of use.

How had such an oasis been a mile from my place all this time and I didn't even know about it?

"Can I help you?" Behind the counter, a teenage girl looked at me suspiciously—as if I'd just walked into her home instead of a coffee shop and was willing to pay.

"What time are you open 'til?"

"Why?"

Seriously? I don't want to sound old, but this next generation was a little odd.

"Because I want to order a mocha and chill out for a while."

Barista Girl eyed me, obviously trying to figure out if I was lying or not. Who lies about getting a drink in a coffee shop?

"Nine on a Tuesday." She continued the stare. "Are you going somewhere?"

And nosy.

"No." Now I was the one who was feeling a little suspicious.

"Don't you think you're a little dressed up for coffee?"

Well, it was true. "Yes."

"Are you meeting someone?"

"Here?"

"Yes."

"Why?"

"You look like one of those women who's out to meet someone." She leaned over the counter and looked at my shoes. "Are you having an affair?"

"Abby, just give the woman her coffee." The voice was as rich as the coffee beans on the counter without the bitter aftertaste.

I turned, toward the voice, surprised at the guy attached to it. This was not the typical night manager. He was average height, but definitely better looking than average with a kind smile and slightly mussed hair.

"Hi, I'm John." He stuck his hand over the counter. "If you're here to have an affair, I should warn you I had closed-circuit cameras installed after we were robbed this spring."

I didn't feel a flicker when he shook my hand, but it made me wonder why—*why*—had I wasted the last three years with Jason? If there were truly funny, nice, hot guys out there who probably wouldn't leave you stranded in the suburbs…again, I ask you, why?

"I'm not having an affair…sadly." Ain't that the truth? I was like the anti-affair.

John glanced towards Barista Girl and back. "Oddly—and these are words that don't come out of my mouth very often—I have to agree with Abby. You're a little over-dressed to have a coffee by yourself."

"Well, that's what happens when you go for a romantic dinner and end up trapped out there without cab fare."

"Ouch."

Abby slid the mocha across the counter, still looking at me as if I at any second might pull a weapon and rob them.

Instead, I pulled my debit card out, considering a cupcake too, when John shook his head.

"On the house."

This was seriously my new favorite place.

I thanked him and headed for the overstuffed chairs by the fireplace. Glancing at my phone, I couldn't believe it was only seven-fifty. My life completely annihilated in less time than an evening out.

I sipped the mocha—the really good mocha actually—and considered my next move.

I needed a place to live, maybe a car, and a job, like yesterday. Of course, I *had* a job yesterday. Severance was three weeks. Plus the two weeks of vacation time they owed me would give me some breathing room. Not enough for a *deep* breath. Of course, I had the small amount from selling my belongings, but I probably should just buy new belongings. Floors get hard.

"So, Mocha, what's the plan?" John settled into the chair next to me. "You going to just camp out here?"

I could see the guy was actually worried. A complete stranger, worried about my well-being. I couldn't help thinking Jason wouldn't be thinking about if *I* was okay right now, let alone worry about a stranger.

"I'm just working up the balance to walk home. It's going to be a wobbly one in these shoes."

He looked at me, looked at my shoes, looked back up at me.

"My girlfriend is stopping by in a bit if you want a ride. We could drop you off at your place, no problem."

His girlfriend. Figures. More proof all the good ones were taken.

But, I wasn't one to look a gift ride in the mouth.

"That would be great. Really great." I glanced toward Barista Girl. "I don't suppose you could tell her I was having an affair with your girlfriend?"

John grinned. It was amazing how subtle the difference was between a grin and a smirk. How sometimes you could think for years someone was grinning at you and then, in one blow, you begin to wonder if all those looks had been something less nice.

Of course, the universe would place the perfect Jason Foil in front of me to drive home my own purposeful blindness.

"Don't mind Abby. She's in a special work-study program for teens. She's learning management first hand."

"Would this work study program involve checking-in with the warden each night?"

The grin faltered. "Not quite."

I was surprised how closely I must have hit that one.

"Well, good for her. She's doing better than I am."

"Hey, one bad night isn't the end of the world."

"So true. It's the no-job-lease-ending-getting-dumped combo that really does a girl in."

"Oh. Again with the ouch."

"I don't suppose you know a great, cheap place that won't need me to have, you know, a job or belongings or a plan?"

John leaned back, glancing around as he thought.

"Maybe." He pulled out his phone and texted someone. "Can you stop by tomorrow? I might have something for you."

I must have looked as shocked as I felt, because John stood and gave me what could only be called a *reassuring smile.*

"Enjoy your mocha. Chill out. Sarah will be here later and we'll deal with everything tomorrow."

Later, when I looked up from one of the used self-help books I'd snagged, a small, curvy blond had her arm wrapped around John's waist. I half expected her to glare at me when he steered them my way, but instead, her smile widened.

"I hear you're having a crappy night."

I laughed. How could I not? She was just as likeable as he was. They were, apparently, Adorable Couple.

"Yup. Pretty much." I pulled my coat on and reached for my tiny purse. "Thanks for the ride."

"No problem. Figured I'll take you home while he closes up." She grabbed her own bag and led the way to the front door. "I hope you like help. John is Mr. Fix It and now that he knows you're looking for a place, he's put on his Wanna-Be Realtor hat."

"I'm not going to argue with anyone's wanna-be anything right now."

"Great. Just don't let him hang anything in your new place." She seemed amazingly adamant about that. I kind of wondered what type of art John had been running around town hanging.

So, I just smiled at that, because who was I to judge anyway?

Maybe things were looking up.

FOUR

THINGS WERE DEFINITELY not looking up.

The next morning, not only was my apartment freezing, but I didn't have hot water. A few weeks ago it would have been just chilly. But, with summer turning into fall, night was still dead cold.

It figures with only one day to go on my lease the building would have a major fail. I called the building manager and wasn't surprised when I got his voicemail.

"Micah? It's Kasey Lane in 304. I'm in my apartment and I have no heat or hot water...Wait." I glanced at my alarm clock. The small battery icon was on. "I also don't have electricity. What exactly is going on? Please call me back."

I wrapped my moss green comforter around me—glad I hadn't donated it or my bed yet even though it didn't play matchy-matchy in Jason's apartment—and headed toward my front door.

The building hallway was nice and toasty...and lit. This was not a good sign.

Beth, the girl across the way, opened her door and caught me standing in the middle of the hall, comforter pulled up around my nose as I tried to get warm.

"No heat or hot water." Check me out. Stater of Things Obvious.

She leaned around me to look into my apartment as if cold air might look different. "Really? Everything's fine in here."

Figures.

Beth gave me a whattayougonnadoaboutit smile and headed out the front door. Also not a surprise. She was the kind of neighbor who stopped by to let you know she was having a big party—but not invite you. Just tell you so you'd know what the noise was.

I hit redial and waited for Micah's voicemail.

"Seriously, Micah. Why is my apartment the only one that's arctic? Call me back. I'm just, you know, hanging out in the hallway in my pajamas."

A door upstairs opened and a heavy footfall crossed over my head toward the stairs. The guy Beth kept calling the cops on for doing P90X after seven on a Saturday turned the corner and stopped on the landing.

"Locked out?" It dawned on me how bad I must look pre-shower, pre-caffeine.

"Nope."

"Just hanging out?" He grinned.

And why shouldn't he. I must look ridiculous. "No heat, hot water, or electricity."

"For real?" He looked at my door as if he could see the problem through the flimsy paneling. "Listen, I'm just running out to get coffee and bagels, but my girlfriend is here for the weekend. Why don't you grab your stuff and go shower at my place. She won't care."

Dan—which was apparently P90X guy's name—brought me up, introduced me to his girlfriend, and headed for the door.

It showed how low I'd sunk that I didn't even care I was showering in some strange guy's apartment. Dan's girlfriend grabbed me a towel and made sure I had everything I needed.

"Lucky for you he hires a maid service the week before I come to visit. I'm deathly afraid of what you'd find otherwise."

"Thanks." I tried to imagine Dan—who always looked amazingly put together—having a filthy bathroom. It just didn't compute.

But, who was I to try to read someone else's boyfriend when I hadn't even been able to read my own?

I hurried through my shower not wanting to cut into the Dan-Girlfriend time. Plus, I had a date with a coffee shop owner who was hopefully finding me a roof to live under. I was not above begging at this point.

I dried my hair as quickly as possible and wrapped it up in a sloppy bun before thanking them both, a little sad to meet the nice neighbor the day before I moved out.

Back in Antarctica, I opened my shades to let the sunshine in before I wrapped a scarf around my neck, pulled on my coat, and hefted my tote. How had I never noticed how heavy it was with the laptop and charger when I was only walking a block to the bus stop?

I may not have a check paying out for today, but it was still a work day. I had a lot of work and even more thinking to do. I might as well get started.

The air was damp, the type of pre-fall weather that made everything feel a bit more crisp. It was a shorter walk than expected. More like three-quarters of a mile. That's what happened when you stayed in your own neighborhood—you missed out on hidden gems.

I slipped into the café and breathed in that heady coffee-air. Being there again was the first thing that felt good—that felt right—in two days.

I stepped up to the counter, happy to get another one of those to-die-for mochas and oddly unsurprised to find Abby manning the counter again.

She looked at me and shook her head. "This is how you leave the house?"

I looked down at my yoga pants and North Face jacket.

"Yes. This is how I leave the house when I need to walk a mile to sit and sip coffee while working."

She shook her head again, disgust emanating off her like she'd just discovered I kicked kittens as a hobby.

"If you insist on going out like that, you're going to stay single."

"I've only been single since last night—you know, when you accused me of being an adulteress."

"Yup. Welcome to Singleland." Abby handed me my mocha as if it was above my touch. "You'll be here a while."

"Maybe I'd like to be single a while."

She looked at me over the mist from the steamer. "You don't seem like someone who likes being single." With that, she headed down the counter to wipe off some machine.

I stared after her wondering if she was right. Was I that girl who didn't like to be single? Was I? Was that why I'd stayed with Jason?

I didn't think so, but there was a lot I was learning about myself this week.

I settled into the same overstuffed chair as the night before and pondered. I was definitely in a pondering place in life.

Once I pushed aside the Singleland pondering, I started considering the real issue at hand. In the back of my mind, I had an idea—one that had lived there for a while trying to work up the courage to pop out. But now, in a mental fight-or-flight situation, it pushed its way to the front and itched at my brain since I'd woken up cold and annoyed.

My own marketing and design business. Promo, websites, banners, ads. Lots of fun designs to do on my own. No big corporate accounts arguing over what such-and-such shade of orange subconsciously says. Just straightforward work for startups, individuals, and small companies.

Affordable but gorgeous work.

I had the skills. I had the drive.

Looking through my contacts, I tried to figure out where I might find a couple clients to kick off my new business once I got it up and running. I wasn't sure where the ethical line was about contacting former clients. One thing I did know about myself, that wasn't a line I would cross.

Obviously I'd need something to show them. Something as good as what I'd been able to do with resources, but on a much smaller budget. What could I offer that would make me stand out? That would make me a success? That would allow me to pay the rent?

I Googled designers and started grabbing screenshots. I pulled out my Moleskin and made notes of different things offered, pricing, timelines, color schemes, websites…anything that someone else was doing. I marked examples up. I made notes of what could be done better, different, or just more *me*.

It was fun. It was exciting. But, it was just the start and when I tried to think beyond that, I got a little freaked out.

After an hour I'd gone through my mocha. Another one was definitely needed to tackle a business plan while I waited for John.

And lucky for me, Abby was still working the counter.

"You know what your problem is?" she started before I could even get my order out.

"No, but I'm sure that as my local barista there's nothing you'd like more than to tell me."

It's a sad state of affairs when I didn't feel odd or guilty verbally sparring with a child.

"Look at you. You're a mess."

I glanced down. Probably out of habit. Abby may have started channeling my mother. Was I a mess? Emotionally or physically? She probably meant a little bit of both.

"That's not good." She said it as if being a mess was occasionally a good thing and I might be confused. "It's hard enough being a girl, let alone an average girl. But you're lowering your own social credit-rating coming in here like this."

I shouldn't ask. It was a dumb move and I knew it even as the question slipped past my lips. "Social credit-rating?"

"I call it the Average Girl Theory. It's the reason you're single and don't know what to do about it."

I knew what to do about it: Nothing.

I'd been single—I glanced at my watch—fourteen hours. I hadn't dropped dead from lack of a man in my life yet.

I was more than not-dead. I was feeling pretty darn good.

When I'd decided to move in with Jason, my mother hadn't been happy. Too many milk-cow references to count. My aunts joined in. The happily-marrieds joined forces to try to talk me out of it. No one, not one person just came out and said they didn't like him. They just thought we should get married instead of moving in together.

Or maybe they didn't like him.

But this—this underage, self-proclaimed love guru—was too much.

"See, guys are very visual." Barista Girl Abby nodded as if I wasn't going to believe her or this was—I don't know—*news.* "Everything is about what they can see. They can't *see* that you're smart or funny or whatever your I Am Woman thing is. It's all about the visual."

"So you said." I couldn't be blamed if that sounded dry even to me.

"Now you come in here looking like that." She waved her hand vaguely at me from her side of the counter. "Not good."

"Last night you accused me of being an adulteress."

I was really beginning to wish I hadn't given her money. Or that she'd already given me my mocha. Or that my ego wasn't taking a hit for no apparent reason.

Or...or...or...

Ah, the fabulous life of the newly single girl. The single *average* girl apparently.

Of course, I hadn't dressed up to walk here and work all day. Yoga pants and a fitted t-shirt were as good as it was going to get. I'd already planned to bring my entire business wardrobe to a consignment shop to help make another rent check happen.

Of course, designer clothes and toe-pinching shoes were a corner I didn't mind cutting.

Now I just needed a rent to pay.

I picked at the small hole starting to fray along the edge of my t-shirt and reminded myself the last thing I needed right now was another guy. I was done being any-type-of-maintenance and was moving on to Independent Business Woman.

Barista Girl caught my eye as I finished inspecting my can-this-shirt-be-saved inspection.

"Maybe a little makeup too. You know. Just some mascara and gloss."

"Is my mocha done?" Really. Did she think this was the way to a big tip—annoy the patrons into paying her to leave them alone?

I shook my change purse. It was probably too light to afford that blessing.

"Not yet." She glanced down at the empty to-go cup in her hand. "So, the theory. Guys. They rate themselves very high while knocking women down easily. So, let's assume about eighty-five percent of the women fall into that average looks group. Some are rated higher, upper-average—like upper-middle class—and some are ranked lower on the scale. But they all fall into the middle of the bell curve."

I glanced at her hand, the one with my empty cup, waiting for her to finish so I could get back to work. I had a company to launch.

"Anyway," she continued, setting my still-empty cup down. "Guys don't live on the same bell curve. When they see that ten percent of really gorgeous hot girls, seventy percent of guys think that girl is obtainable. That seventy percent is cutting into the equivalent AGQ—Average Girl Quotient—by quite a bit. Think about it. If a guy who ranks as a six thinks he can date a nine, who are the sixes going to date?"

It frightened me that she was actually making sense.

More than frightened. I glanced outside to see if there were any other signs of the apocalypse approaching.

"So, all those upper-average guys think they rate an above-average girl."

"What about the other thirty percent of men?" What was I thinking? Where had the little voice that lived in my head gone? It should be shouting, *Do not engage! Do not engage!*

"Well the lowest portion—the *below* average men—realize where they stand. They've accepted they're in the bottom fifteen percent and have found a girl at their attraction level. Think about it. You see a girl. You know you're *way* prettier than she is, but she has a boyfriend. Usually we don't stop and think, *Yeah. But I wouldn't date him.* We just get stuck on the *she has a boyfriend and I don't* thing."

Who sounded bitter now, Barista Girl?

"That still leaves about fifteen percent of guys." Why was I torturing myself like this?

"Yup." Barista Girl nodded her head. "You're absolutely right. And most of them are taken. They were smart. They grabbed a great girl and they're keeping her. The rest of them are just figuring it out. You better hope you get your act together and stay roughly an eight before you age out."

Age out?

I was twenty-six. What exactly was I aging out of?

"Can I have my drink?"

The snap in my voice must have finally been obvious because she made a face and started doing whatever it was they did behind the counter to create that mocha magic. I had better enjoy it now. With my new lack of income, these weren't going to be in the necessities column where they used to reside.

Once Theory Creating Barista Girl finished my frothy goodness, I grabbed a napkin and headed back to my desk—comfy chair and coffee table—in the corner.

"Don't listen to her." The voice was soft, kind of lifting on the end. It matched the girl in an odd sort of way. She had to be about my age, with light brown hair framing a glasses covered pixie face.

"Sorry?"

"Don't listen to her. She's wrong." The girl glanced toward the counter before shifting in her chair to look at me. "Okay, she may not be wrong. The theory probably holds. But she's like nine years old and you can't put a number on some things."

"I'd like to hope that's true." Especially since I wasn't looking so good on paper at this point. There was nothing attractive about homelessness. One more reason I had to get this business up and running.

The whole idea that I had to *carry my own weight* had ticked me off last night. There was a reason "for better or for worse" was in the marriage vows. But that was in a *real* relationship. Not one you thought was real but apparently was just a convenience to one party. One more reason Jason and I weren't married. And now, there's no way I'd be putting myself out there when I was homeless and unemployed.

Of course, there was no way I'd be putting myself out there for quite a while anyway. I was pretty much declaring the ten foot sphere around me a Guy Free Zone. I might even bring back the giant hoop skirts to enforce this new sanction.

But, she wasn't done.

"My boyfriend, Ben?" She got this silly grin on her face. "He's gorgeous. Like, the second most beautiful guy I know. Seriously. Do I look like beautiful guy material?"

I almost shook my head. Not because she wasn't pretty. She was. In a cute, girl-next-door-who-is-a-bit-too-nerdy way. I was pretty sure guys would be attracted to her just because of all that shininess coming off her. And the glasses. I'd never been envious of girls with glasses, but she seemed to pull them off as if they were just part of her look.

Of course, that could just be New Relationship Shine, but I was guessing she was pretty darn adorable sans-Ben.

"I'm Jenna Drake." She leaned over the coffee table, hand stretched out.

It was such a welcoming gesture. She just wasn't one of those people you dismissed rudely because you were trying to work. Plus, her name was vaguely familiar as I struggled to place it. I was really, *really* hoping we hadn't gone to high school together or something.

That was the last thing I needed. The small town gossip tree was still alive and well. My mother would have me on the phone thirty seconds after she heard my new status, and I'd be getting a lecture on women alone in the world.

Obviously my mother had accidentally time warped to the 1940s.

In her eyes, there was only one thing worse than not being married…being single.

"Kasey Lane."

"Oh!" She pulled out a little red notebook and scribbled in it. "That's a great name. I'm totally stealing it."

Stealing my name? As in identity theft? I wasn't sure what else she could mean, but she didn't have any of my information so figured I was fairly safe. I'd just have to remember not to leave my purse alone…or throw my receipt away.

She glanced up and must have caught the horrified look on my face.

"Oh, don't worry. I'm not stealing anything *real*. Just your name. It's a great name," she said again, this time with a smile as she folded the notebook back into her tote. "I'm a writer and you'd be shocked how hard it gets to come up with new names. I mean, there's what? Millions of them? And yet, you find yourself drifting toward the same ones over and over again. I have tried to name four different guys James."

She was a little bundle of energy…really unfocused energy.

"Sorry. I'm trying not to babble. I'm not good with people."

She seemed to really think that. She'd been nothing but sweet, welcoming and friendly. If this was bad with people I was in a lot of trouble.

And Barista Abby…Well, Abby was five steps past trouble. The Brew Ha Ha might need to be reconsidered as my new hangout.

"No. No, that's okay," I jumped in before she could start up again. "I was just a little thrown by the word *steal*. It could be kind of fun to know my name is out there in some book.

Kind of like a famous non-version of me." I could pick the book up and show my girlfriends next time we got together. *Look, this character is named after me!* You don't get that being a soccer mom. Wait. "What exactly did you say you write?"

With my luck she wrote some weird niche-erotica I'd have to deal with every time someone Googled me.

"YA, young adult."

Oh. That sounded fairly safe. It did seem weird they'd let a slightly crazy woman write for kids, but what did I know?

Jenna smiled and began pulling more stuff out of her tote. A laptop and cord, a small giraffe-shaped timer, a pile of scribbled on pages.

"You don't usually work here, do you?" She opened the laptop and leaned back in her chair while it powered up.

"First day. Good mocha."

"That's why you aren't familiar. This is my can't-take-my-own-company-any-longer office." It was hard to dislike a girl who was so kind to others and laughed at herself so easily.

I glanced around. Besides Abby, it was pretty dead. I pulled the overstuffed chair next to me, close enough to strategically pile stuff on it.

"Is it always this quiet?"

"Not usually on Wednesdays. Midweek slump. It must be the nice weather. During the week there's a small lunch rush and then quiet again 'til the after work crowd. John says they're packed during the morning commute, but that would involve getting up before eight, so..."

"Sweet."

"I'll be here every day for a while." She pulled the computer onto her lap and set the timer. "A tree fell into my office."

A tree fell into it? She said it as if this was an everyday occurrence. I almost asked her about it, but she smiled, stuck her earbuds in, and began typing away.

It took me a moment to refocus, which was weird since I'd been so surprised she'd sat in my overstuffed corner of the café and chatted me up.

Hopefully nothing fell on her while we were working so close together. She seemed like the type of person something like that would happen to.

And my luck didn't need any help getting worse.

FIVE

I SHOULD HAVE known you guys would find each other." John's voice cut through the music I'd plugged in to drown out my thoughts. There was nothing like a little Jason Aldean to get you rocking out when you didn't want to think about life. I was ignoring that his name was *Jason* and focusing on the *Country Rock God* part of the equation.

I pulled my earbuds out and looked up at him resting on the edge of the arm of Jenna's chair.

"Who?"

If this was another attempt at telling me how to meet men, I was going to have to rethink this whole place, mocha thing or not.

"You and Jenna. Jenna's the one we need to ask about the apartment."

I turned toward the adorable elf half-hidden behind the seventeen inch screen of her laptop.

"You're moving?"

Her cheerfulness seemed a little droopy as she shook her head.

"Not me. Ben is going to London for a year and was thinking about subletting his apartment."

Wow. In some ways that was worse than being dumped. At least I could get over my ex-idiot. I felt like I was most-of-the-way there already. But, if someone I really loved was going away for twelve months...Yeah, that kind of stunk. A lot.

"So, he's just looking to sublet it?"

Jenna nodded. "Maybe. He wasn't sure. The company is paying for his place in London, so it's not like he's losing out. But it makes sense to have someone in there."

I thought about the overly-charming neighborhood we were currently in and my lack of charming-level money.

"Is it near here? I probably can't afford anything in this neighborhood." I was getting tired of my own tale of woe at this point. "I lost my job and was supposed to be moving in with my boyfriend—now *ex*-boyfriend—this weekend so, rent is going to be tight as it is. I have five weeks' payout and some savings, but I don't want to get into a bad situation money-wise."

"Well, he's coming in this afternoon. We can ask him what he's looking for when he gets here. How much furniture do you have?"

"As of tomorrow?" I couldn't believe the spot I'd gotten myself into. That I'd allowed Jason to paint me into it. "Basically nothing."

Jenna and John looked at me as if I'd just told them I was forced to put down my dog...You know, the one I don't have who peed on my rug I no longer own.

"It's a long story," I explained, hoping I wouldn't have to explain. "Filled with woe and much Craigslist-ing."

"Okay." Jenna had pulled out her phone and was texting before she'd even answered.

"So, Kasey. What's the plan?" John settled himself into the chair next to Jenna and took a sip of whatever the great smelling thing was in his cup.

"The plan?"

"The get-life-back-on-track plan."

Oh. That.

I considered dodging the question, but since today was my first official day of being self-employed, I should probably share that.

"I'm starting my own business."

"Really?" He sounded a little worried. Which, since he was a business owner, I found ironic. And worrisome.

"Yup. I'm a graphic designer. I've done a ton of marketing campaigns. I thought I'd rather do it on my own and work with a smaller clientele base than run big, corporate projects anymore." Plus that whole, *lost my job* thing.

Jenna glanced up, studying me. For the first time I saw someone who wasn't flaky. Someone who knew what she was doing.

"Do you have any samples of your work?"

Darn it. Samples. I hadn't gotten that far.

"I'm doing some market analysis first to see what smaller groups and individuals would most likely be interested in and are able to afford. But, if you're curious…" I scribbled down five of the last websites I'd done in conjunction with a marketing plan. "I did the pitch and saw all of these projects through."

Jenna took the paper and typed the first one in. I watched her—nose scrunched up, eyes focused—as she paged through the first site.

"How much direction did they give you?"

"It depends on the client. Sometimes they have no idea what they want. Sometimes they have *a vision*." I grinned, thinking of my last job with a lawyer who thought he was a closet artist. "Occasionally the vision is actually doable. I have a questionnaire for them either way that helps get things clear on both sides."

I scribbled down *questionnaire* on my to do list. I better have those ready to go. And business cards. And my own website. And a brand. You know, nothing too time consuming.

I mentally did the how-much-money-is-in-my-bank-account math, glad I could do the work on my own.

Jenna nodded again. "Let me look at these. I may have some more questions."

I glanced toward John, unsure what was going on, but pretty stoked. If I was reading the situation right, I might have my first client.

"You ladies enjoy the beverages." He rose, lifting his empty mug as he went. "I have to go manage something."

A glance back at Jenna showed me I should let her be. One thing I'd learned working in a corporate setting was when to let the client think.

And, if I was going to have a client, I had a couple things to do. I glanced at my to do list pretending it could all get done in one afternoon. After all, ignorance, even denial-style, was bliss.

S I X

HEY THERE, SUNSHINE. Creating worlds to rip apart?"

That had to be Ben. Not just because he'd pulled a chair practically into her lap and kissed her forehead as he sat, but because I could easily believe he was the second most gorgeous guy in town.

And smitten. He was totally smitten.

"I've just added a car accident while the driver was texting. Only, I'm not sure it's funny enough."

I wasn't sure it was funny at all, but what did I know?

"I mean," she continued. "It's a serious topic, but it still has to be funny."

Ben nodded his head as if this was a normal conversation.

"Oh. Ben!" Jenna closed her laptop and motioned toward me. "This is Kasey Lane. Is that not one of the best names ever?"

Ben offered me his hand and a smile that told me he was humoring her—but not by much. I couldn't imagine finding a guy who saw my best in what others saw as a bit odd.

"Ben Donahue."

"Kasey of the awesome name."

He flashed that grin at me and I didn't blame Jenna one bit for her smittenness. Where she was all nerdy-glasses girl, he was hot JCrew glasses guy. They'd have the most adorable near-sighted children ever.

"So, Ms. Awesome Name, I hear you're looking for a new place to live."

It was embarrassing. More than embarrassing. But, what are you going to do about. It was true, I was desperate, and he might be the answer.

I gave him the basics: Lost job, new company, bad break-up, the end.

"Guys can be the ruination of all things good. I'm a guy and I'm still only running fifty-percent in that category."

"Fifty-percent?"

"My two best guy friends. One is a womanizer and one's trying to save the world."

"I didn't know the two were mutually exclusive." I slapped a hand over my mouth. Nothing like insulting the guy's friend while asking for a favor.

Ben laughed. "Okay. True enough. But Max is a good guy. He was my roommate in college. Dane, well…Women think he's pretty. We'll leave it at that. I figure they cancel each other out."

Jenna shut her laptop and set it aside. "You'll like Max. You'll like Dane too. It's nearly impossible not to once you can hear him talking through the blinding good-looks that dull all your senses."

That was all I needed—more womanizing men. They probably had Convenience Girlfriends who didn't push for a commitment when they'd been seeing each other for years…or, you know, were moving in together.

"So, here's the deal. I have a place about two blocks from here. I'll be gone for about a year." He reached out and wrapped Jenna's hand in his. "When I come back to visit, I might want to get into my storage closet, but I'd just stay with Jenna if she doesn't have any more natural disasters at her place. I'd feel good having someone in there. Knowing there won't be any issues with frozen pipes or break-ins this winter. I was thinking this would be a win-win."

Two blocks away was way too close to super-nice territory. I was pretty sure I wasn't going to be able to afford even a win-win price—until he named it.

"You can't be serious. You could get double that."

Ben shrugged. "I don't need the money because of the job set up. My mortgage is low and that's us splitting it in half. I thought you might want to come see it today."

"After lunch. You'll have to sit through a meal with us while I grill you about your new company and the huge favor you're going to do for me in exchange for living at my boyfriend's place."

I'll be honest, that statement—even said in her perky little voice—made me a little nervous.

Jenna went back to typing away while Ben and I chatted. It felt awkward hanging out with her guy.

"Don't mind her. She'll stay in her own world until she gets to a good stopping place."

With a snap, she finally closed the laptop. "I'm ready for lunch any time you are."

Somehow she made this sound as if she'd just been waiting on us.

"Of course you are. But, Kasey was trying to get some work done." Ben leaned over and kissed her lightly before glancing at me with a grin. "We're working on awareness."

"I'm perfectly aware. I'm just hungry."

"Well, we can get you a snack if it will keep you being nice to our company." Ben leaned back in his chair, watching Jenna pack up her stuff.

Jenna looked grim. You'd think Ben had been starving her. "Maybe just a small snack. I mean, because we have to wait then walk to the restaurant and then wait. It makes sense."

"Of course it does." Ben gave me a grin as he rose and headed toward the counter. "Never get between Jenna and her computer or food. Otherwise, she's pretty easygoing."

Good to know.

I was about to comment on Jenna's tiny waist versus her not-so-tiny appetite, but instead figured it was probably best to wrap up my research so we could get the girl to a restaurant.

If food was the way to Jenna's heart and Jenna was the way to Ben's apartment, I could get us to a lunch spot faster than a womanizing ass could dump a relationship-blind girl.

SEVEN

B EN'S APARMENT WAS everything a girl could
dream of. Settled on the top floor of an old
brownstone walk-up, it had a tiny "terrace" that
was basically the roof of the floor below, a breakfast nook
with a big window, and a small, but comfortably furnished
living room. The kitchen was small, but had a raised
microwave to save counter space—and my ability to feed
myself. The bedroom hooked off the living room and
squeezed into a corner surrounded by windows was a cute
little desk.

I could live here. I could even work here.

"You can see most of my mortgage is location." Ben gave
a little self-deprecating grin. "It's so small I've learned to keep
it clean. Even a sock on the floor makes everything feel
cluttered. The building has rules about everything, so it's
better to have someone here. But, it's a great space and I
don't want to have to sell it."

If this was mine, I'd never want to lose it either.

"You're really willing to sublet it to me at that rate?"

"I wasn't going to sublet it at all. The company that's hired my group is going to board us in London. Now I won't have to worry if something happens in the building, and I can to afford to come home more often." Ben wrapped an arm around Jenna. "You can see where that would be a draw."

I did another lap around the place, as if there was a decision to make.

"I can't thank you enough for this. Jason gave me back my first rent and half my security deposit so I can write you a check today if you'd like."

"He gave you back *half* your security?" Jenna all but stuck her hands on her hips as she said it.

"I know. I just didn't know what to say when it happened. He gave it to me in a Hallmark card."

"Oh! What did the card say?" Jenna had that gleam in her eye that was becoming familiar. She was probably the most curious person I'd ever met.

"Jenna, not everyone wants to share every detail of their personal life."

"Actually…" I dug in my bag looking for the envelope. "I haven't even opened it yet."

"You didn't check that the money was all there?"

"Well, I figured who lies about giving you back only half your money."

We all looked at the envelope as if it was going to start talking.

"Well." Jenna bounced on her toes. "Open it."

"Sunshine." Ben obviously spent a lot of time gently reining her in.

"No. Let's open it." I tore the corner and stuck my finger in, running it across the top until I could pull the check out of the card. The check was there for exactly the amount he told me it would be worth. "All there."

"Read the card."

"Jenna Jameson Drake." Ben took her by the shoulders and turned her away from me so she'd—hopefully—lose her focus. "Maybe she wants to ritualistically burn the card without having ever read it."

"Oh, that's good." I started considering the places a fire could be built without getting the fire department called. "You're good at this. You must have been a woman in a past life."

"I'm secure enough in my manhood to accept that as a compliment."

Ok, here goes. I pulled the card out and examined it.

"There's a cat on the cover. He's wearing a top hat." I held it up so they could see the outside. "And inside..."

I flipped the card open and saw...Nothing. Not one thing. He'd given me a blank card and hadn't even signed it.

"Wow. That's—I don't even have words." Jenna just stared at the card. "It's not very often I don't have any words. But this may be one of those times."

We all just stared at the card.

Just stared as if the longer we looked the more the chance of it making sense might happen.

"Do you think he just had this sitting around the house?"

Yesterday I would have said no. But, today I was realizing anything Jason-related was possible.

"Maybe? Who knows?" But, at that point, I didn't even care. I was only going to be homeless for a few weeks and I had a great business plan forming. Maybe getting dumped was the universe forcing me to shake loose all the bad stuff in my life. "I'd love to sublet this place."

"Great!" Ben wrapped an arm around Jenna again. "Looks like you're going to be stuck with me every night for the next three weeks."

"Oh. Wow. I don't want to force you out of your house."

"Don't worry about it. I mean, why move twice? And where would you go for three weeks anyway? As long as you don't mind that we can make some time each weekend for me to do some long term packing. We'll make it work."

"Isn't he the best?" Jenna beamed up at him. No wonder she seemed like she was always so happy.

"Guys. This is too much. This is great." I fought the tears I hadn't cried since this all started two days before. "I just can't believe this."

"No worries." Ben shifted one foot behind the other, leaning away, obviously uncomfortable with the near tears. "Why don't you go home and get yourself ready to move tomorrow? We'll trade physical labor. I'll help you get stuff in and you'll help me get stuff out."

And with that, I headed back to my empty, cold, dark apartment to get ready to move into a cozy little paradise.

EIGHT

IGHT CALLS. I'd called Micah eight times. He hadn't returned them when I'd reported my heat-hot-water-electric issue. Not when I'd called to see when they were going to be back on. Not when I'd called to say I'd be moving out on the agreed upon date and needed a parking pass for a moving van. And not when I'd called while walking back.

By the time I'd run all my errands and headed home it was dark out and I was getting chilly and annoyed. Plus, I really had no interest in sleeping in a cold, dark room again.

I climbed the three flights to my apartment and slid the key home into the lock.

Nothing.

I checked the number on the door. Yup, I lived there. I pulled the key out and tried it again. Nope. Still didn't turn.

I rooted around for my cell phone and checked my messages. Nothing. Not one thing. Who doesn't call back a tenant in an emergency?

I considered calling him one more time, but figured he'd just ignore me again. Micah had never been the best super in the world, but I'd never thought he'd lock me out of my own apartment.

On the upside, I always left my bedroom window cracked. Jason had told me over and over again that it was a bad idea. That I should at least get a bar to block the window from opening more since the fire escape landing was right outside.

I kept meaning to. I kept forgetting.

Now, that meant I had another way into my apartment.

I tromped back downstairs and out the front door. On the sidewalk, I glanced up to Micah's apartment, but the light was out. Without any other options, I headed around to the side of the building to begin my MacGyver entry.

The first step was just getting onto the fire stairs. It took several tries to jump high enough to loop my bag's strap over the first rung of the stairs and pull them down. Then, it flew up, clanging against the landing above it when I tried to unhook my bag. I was making such a racket even the stray cats were taking off.

After two more tries, the bag was looped over my shoulder and the ladder was firmly in hand. I climbed up the cold, rusty metal, inching by dark windows and hoping I didn't scare poor Mrs. Windsor on the second floor. All I needed was to try to explain her heart attack to her children.

When I got to the landing outside my bedroom, I tried to wedge the tips of my fingers into the small space between the window and the outside sill. Since I barely opened the window, they barely fit. It took all my strength to open it from the odd angle, working one side and then the other. And I still couldn't really fit my fingers through.

What I needed was a crowbar or something I could slide into that tiny spot.

And Jason was convinced it would be easy to break in and rob me.

With a relieved sigh, the window gave and opened just enough for me to slip inside. I dropped the bag in and then crouched to follow it, leaning in and placing my hands on the floor as I scooted through like an oversized worm.

When I reached my butt, I was sure for a moment I wasn't going to fit. Who knows how I'd have backed out of that? Just as I slipped through, I felt a spiky scrape on my leg and a yank on my pants as they got caught on something sharp outside on the fire escape.

After a few tugs—and a few shakes—it became obvious I wasn't getting out of this without ripping my favorite yoga pants.

On the upside, no one was around to see me get out of this without my dignity instead.

I turned on my side, resting on my head and shoulder on the floor. Clearly I was going to have one heck of a crink in my neck the next morning. With my free hand, I worked at my yoga pants until I could shove them down with my feet. When they were almost off, they caught on my shoes, so I toed those off onto the fire escape. As soon as I was free, I slid all the way in, pushed the window open, and reached out to grab my shoes, searching for them in the darkness.

It wasn't until I spotted them that I realized a beam of light was coming from behind me.

"Just ease back in the window and turn around slowly," the deep voice commanded.

I glanced over my shoulder and could see two men silhouetted by the light from the building's hallway, but everything else was blinded by the flashlight aimed at my face.

My hesitation must have annoyed him, because the voice came with an edge this time. "Ma'am you're going to have to come back in. We'll talk about this. Calmly."

"Who are you?"

"Officer Darby. I'm going to have to ask you to raise your hands and turn around slowly."

Oh my goodness. I was hanging out the window with my butt covered only by my haven't-been-packed-yet panties. Not to mention the police had managed to get into my apartment when I hadn't been able to. How the heck had that happened?

I slid back in, wishing I could melt through the floor, and turned to face them, my yoga pants held up as a shield in front of me.

"You're going to have to drop the pants and come this way."

"Why are you in my apartment?" I wasn't dropping the pants even for the cops.

"It's not your apartment," a second voice whined. "You moved out."

I raised my hand to shade my eyes from the light. "Micah?"

"She moved out."

"Sir, it doesn't look like Ms. Lane moved out."

"She gave me notice."

"For the end of the month. Which isn't until tomorrow."

Forget divinity. I needed pants. I hitched one leg up and pulled my yoga pants on, then repeated the process with the other leg without turning around or bending over.

"I called you nine times today. First about my heat being off. Then about my electric and hot water. Then just to try to find you. You couldn't return a call but you could get the police here and the door open before I could even climb through my window."

"I didn't want you robbing the place."

"Of what?" I shouted. I was sick of this. Sick of the whole darn week. My high from finding a place to live was pretty much gone. "My own bed? My clothes? Maybe I'd steal my used toothbrush."

"Ms. Lane, you're understandably upset. You're having quite the week."

"That's right I am."

Wait. What?

"First assault. Now breaking and entering. I thought I told you to stay out of trouble."

That sounded vaguely familiar. Hadn't Abby just told me to stay out of trouble? And to make myself dateable. But, on the sliding scale of how much I was willing to listen to her, that advice was pretty low on just about any list I could come up with.

"See?" Micah demanded. "You're going to have to pay for that window."

"Nothing's wrong with the window."

"Then how'd you get in? Huh?" Micah stalked past me and began examining the frame behind me.

Meanwhile, I examined the wide bulk of the silhouette behind the flashlight.

Micah muttered to himself, looking for something wrong with the window. This still wasn't fixing my situation.

"Officer Darby, I have a question." I glanced at Micah over my shoulder, considering pushing him out the window. Besides the law enforcing witness, the idea that the fire escape would stop any type of fall whatsoever ruined the joy I got from the vision. "Isn't it illegal for a landlord to turn off your *paid for* utilities and lock you out of your *paid for* apartment when you have a signed agreement?"

"Actually, it is." I could hear the humor tingeing his voice, a low chuckle closing out the sentence.

"So, not only am I not under arrest, but I might have a case for filing, um, something?"

"Well, not a lot of a case since there were no damages. But you could be a pain about that if you wanted to."

"No. I really just want to sleep somewhere warm, with lights and hot water, my last night here."

Officer Darby lowered the light and I caught a glimpse of a strong jaw and short, dark hair in the dim light. Exactly the kind of guy my friend Jayne would go for. He probably rode a motorcycle and glowered a lot. The kind of guy I avoided at all cost. Definitely not the kind of guy I wanted to keep running into while my life was falling apart.

"I think that's fair. Mr. Marrow, can you get this apartment turned on again?" But, apparently, he was also the voice of reason.

Micah came around to stand beside me and grumbled that he could.

"Within the next thirty minutes?" Officer Darby obviously knew how to ask the right questions.

Micah grumbled under his breath as if I was the person who turned off all my utilities two days early and he had to run around cleaning up my mess.

"So, thanks for coming." I headed toward the door, hoping to walk Officer Darby right past it and push it shut behind him.

"Not so fast, Ms. Lane." The door did fall shut, but Officer Darby was still on my side. "Do you want to explain to me this run of bad luck you seem to be having lately?"

"Not really."

"Do I need to rephrase my question?" He stared down at me, one hand resting casually on the belt above his gun, the other braced on his hip.

"You said I hadn't broken any laws."

"Somehow I suspect you've been bending a few this week." Thank goodness it was dark because I knew he had to be giving me that steely-eyed cop look. He was probably the inscrutable type the actors who played cops studied to be all…inscrutable.

"I really am a law abiding citizen."

I was. I really was. I just wasn't looking so good on my downward spiral.

"This better be the last time I'm called out for you."

"I promise it will be. Nothing else is going to go wrong this week. I've had a distinct run of happy-things since last night."

"Alright." He drew out the word like he didn't believe me. "Just, really, behave yourself."

Officer Darby pulled the door open and I got a peek at sharp, rugged lines, deep blue eyes and jet black hair. I might have been staring a bit. He was only five inches taller than me, but he filled the doorway like it was built around him.

"Also, Ms. Lane?"

"Yes."

"It's Wednesday."

He pulled the door shut behind him as I tried to figure out what that meant. A man of mystery. But, hopefully not one who would be showing up again anytime soon.

Especially not once I moved into Ben's. I had a feeling, climbing half-naked through your own window was even more frowned upon in fancy-shmancy neighborhoods.

NINE

THE LIGHTS WERE still off when the heat kicked in. I lay on my bed listening to the air push through the vents and waiting for it to be warm enough to take my coat off.

You'd think after not having pants on while crawling out of the cool night air and into my own home I'd be...wait a second.

Wednesday.

Every time I thought my humiliation was over for the week, nope. I was pretty sure the underwear I was wearing was dark blue with a bright yellow day of the week across the butt.

Obviously I must be wearing the wrong day.

I spun around chasing my own rear for a moment before flashing myself in the mirror.

Figures.

I was wearing Tuesday.

I listened to the heat clicking on, feeling torn between thankfulness I'd never have to face Officer Darby again and disgust at myself for wishing I'd have to face Officer Darby again. You know, just to look at him. It was nice to see a guy who looked like a guy. I bet Officer Darby didn't own a cashmere sweater.

But, a cop? Talk about the controlling alpha-male stereotype.

No, thank you.

To be fair, he'd handled the situations with both the crazy men in my life with ease and humor. Both of which were things I'd realized I'd been lacking. Not that I needed a hero…I mean, a caregiver.

Whatever.

When the lights came back on, I focused on what needed to be done, packing up the last of my stuff and laying out just what I'd need for the next day.

As I put away the last items, the barren room lost any small amount of charm I'd managed to shove into it. Moving to Ben's cozy haven was going to be a huge upgrade in charm factor.

Slowly, almost as if I were savoring the last night there, I wafted into sleep, glad to be on my own and not managing the emotions of anyone else. I hadn't realized how much I'd had to do that. Jason was temperamental and judgmental and probably just plain mental, but none of that had been obvious to me until it was.

I tried to brush away the feeling of stupidity. But hindsight really was 20-20. Maybe better.

All the what-ifs that led me to dating Jason—the alone in a strange town right after college, a new job, an older guy taking you under his wing—to the reasons I stayed with him—it's what I knew.

After one day as a single girl on the town I felt something I hadn't known I'd lost. A lightness of being. A lack of concern to balance and explain and soften everything going on around me.

I was more than happy with my new situations. I was content. The type of content that lasted.

And I had one person to thank for all that newfound contentedness. Jason.

I'd been blind, but he'd ripped the shades off and pushed me into the world. And it was a much better world without him—even if I had managed to basically flash a cop.

TEN

I WOKE UP TO the sound of my alarm clock, the feel of warm air, and the fulfilled dream of a warm shower awaiting me in my own bathroom.

It was heaven.

I stripped the bed and put the sheets in the laundry basket by the door. This was good-bye. Not that I minded. Evacuating the cookie cutter apartment and getting to spend a year in the old-school charm of the apartment waiting for me a few neighborhoods over was probably going to spoil me for life.

And yet, just like anytime you leave something behind, it all felt very bittersweet. Even the six block walk to the rental place to get a moving van was a journey in good-bye. Farewell, broken sidewalk! So long, crosswalk no one ever stopped at! Arrivederci, takeout Italian bakery!

You'd think I was moving to Paris, not two neighborhoods over.

After maneuvering the rental van back to my place, I brought the rest of my boxes down, shoved them in the back, and headed toward Ben's place ready to grab my keys and kick him out. Nicely, of course, since he was so great. Not to mention my new landlord.

Jenna waved from where she waited on the curb, a spot in front of her filled with two lawn chairs. I'll be honest. I would have paid good money to see Jenna fighting off a parker. I'm not sure if she had a dark side, but I seriously doubt that's what would have brought it out.

I pulled up alongside the spot as she folded the lawn chairs, leaned them against a tree, and eyed it to see if the van would fit.

I'll never understand parallel parking. How many hours of your life are wasted because of it? First you have to find the spot and calculate if you fit. Once you're reasonably sure that you can shove a few tons of metal between two immovable objects, you have to wait until the guy who wasn't paying attention and pulled up on your rear bumper even though you have your reverse lights *and* your directional on smartens up and goes around. Then it takes at least two tries to get in right—four if you're someone who doesn't usually drive.

Hours. Hours of life wasted in which I could be doing something more exciting.

Like napping.

Unfortunately, living in town meant parallel parking. I probably hadn't attempted it in over a year. And that would have been in the tiny Zip Car I'd rented to go holiday shopping last winter.

This wasn't going to be pretty.

I backed the van up a little, and then realized I was at the wrong angle. Pulling out of the spot, I eyed it again to decide my best approach. Edging further into the lane, I watched the bumpers in front and behind me. Then carefully, carefully I backed up. Front bumper. Back bumper in my side mirror. Front bumper. Back bumper in my side mirror. Everything was going fine until Jenna started shouting and waving her arms.

I went to slam my foot on the break, but hit the gas. The rear wheel jumped the curb and I banged into one of the old oaks lining the road.

"Stop!" Jenna looked panicked. She rushed to the back of the van as I eased it out of the spot and put on the hazard lights.

Going around to join her, I eyed the car behind me's bumper to make sure I hadn't managed to ding it too. Thank goodness I'd somehow stayed clear of the sleek urban tank a soccer mom probably drove twice a year.

Jenna stood next to the tree, her hands holding bark onto a small two inch area as if she could repair it just by thinking good thoughts. In the scheme of things, the damage to the tree was minor, but in this neighborhood I wondered if it was the equivalent of murder.

As Jenna focused on healing the tree, I checked out the van's bumper. It had almost no damage. There were some smudges, but when I rubbed the cuff of my sweatshirt over them, they basically disappeared.

"Don't worry. We can fix this!" She shouted because volume always equals truth.

"How?" Unless, she really was a fairy. I glanced toward her again. Probably too tall…and, you know, too human.

I'm not sure how she thought we could fix a tree, but I was willing to let her try since the flip side was the fact that I'd killed city property.

"I don't know. But Ben will. He can fix anything." She turned and sprinted into the building as I stood next to the kitty-corner van and damaged oak.

"What exactly is going on here?"

I knew that voice. It was beginning to signal every disaster I'd had recently. Even coated in liquid chocolate, I knew the sound meant nothing good.

There, of course, was Officer Darby.

And, sadly, there really was no way out of this. I might as well just face it head on. "I, um, may have backed into that tree."

"Ms. Lane, you either backed into town property or you didn't. Which is it?"

"Yes." My shoulders sag. I was pretty much feeling done with disasters. "I backed into town property."

This was not what I needed. I needed a break, not an arrest record.

"Are you following me?" Because, what else could explain this? Maybe that search I'd done for the non-profit group's marketing plan had gotten me onto the NSA. Now they'd assigned an agent to me in local blues.

"Like that's what I want to do with my day off. Follow around a walking felony waiting to happen." He pulled his aviators down his nose to look at me over the top of the rim. "No offense, Tuesday. You're cute and all, but the last thing I need is a woman whose idea of staying out of trouble is duct taping public property back together."

Walking felony? An angry heat rushed over my skin, crushing out my common sense.

"As if I need a smirky-smirky cop doing that outdated Tom Cruise sunglasses move." I glared at him waiting for him to move by. Waiting for him to get out of my day.

"Tom Cruise, huh?" More of the smirky-smirky.

"Don't flatter yourself. I said the move, not the man."

"Either way, you've just damaged a two-hundred and fifty year old oak tree that belongs to the city. What are you going to do about it?"

I felt horrible about the tree. If Jenna hadn't tried to make it sound like no big deal, I probably would have called city hall myself to figure out what to do. But, with Officer Darby standing there basically threatening me, I suddenly felt as if nothing I could do would be the right thing.

"Fine. Arrest me." I stuck my hands out together, offering him my wrists to cuff. "Go ahead. It's your day off. I'm sure the paperwork, let alone the fact that you busted a tree-denter, would really make your day. They'd love that at the station, wouldn't they?"

He didn't even bat an eye, which convinced me he'd never had any intention of doing anything beyond harassing me. He just leaned against that poor tree and crossed his arms, staring at me in that impenetrable way cops on TV all seem to have.

He was trying to break me. I was strong and resilient. I was not going to break. I was—

"Don't you ever go off duty?" I broke. "Did someone assign you to follow me around making sure every transgression was weighed and measured? Is every bad event in my life now accompanied by the threat of imprisonment?"

"When have I ever threatened you with imprisonment?"

"Aren't you about to?" I glanced toward the tree, its scraped bark damning me. "I hit the tree." I shouted a bit irrationally. "I hit the tree and look at it! And the rental van. And now we're not going to be able to move me in and Ben out and I'm really not going to have electricity and heat and I'll be sleeping in the van I'm afraid to return because I scuffed the bumper. Or prison. With women named Tulula."

"Tulula?"

"Oh, shut up. Do whatever you're going to do. I'm just—"

Jenna came storming down the stairs and cut between me and Officer Darby. "What's going on here?"

"Damaged city property." Officer Darby looked her over as if she were the least of his worries. And, she probably was. I mean what could she possibly—

Jenna hauled off and punched Officer Darby square in the chest.

He didn't even flinch. Just looked down at the spot like she'd poked him with a finger.

I sucked in a breath, shocked how quickly this had spiraled out of control. I really was going to end up in prison at this rate.

She went to hit him again and I jumped between them. "Don't do it. It's assaulting an officer."

"It's assaulting an idiot. Max, apologize to Kasey right now."

Max?

"Now, Max." Jenna looked like she was going to hit him again. "The guys are not going to see the humor in this. And, as soon as I get my phone, you will not like the Officer Darby hashtag of the day. You will regret every stupid guy move you've ever made in your life."

Officer Darby—Max, apparently—looked panicked.

"Ms. Lane. I'm sorry. I didn't mean to really upset you. I *am* off duty. We don't need to do anything about the tree. We'll just…fix it." He looked at Jenna. "Right? We can fix it. Just, for crying out loud, not another freaking Officer Darby thing."

"I don't know, Max. Those are my most popular tweets. You have a following. The only thing I can promise is that if you stop being a mean jerk right now, there won't be any hashtag backlash."

Max was already nodding. "Fine, but Jenna, you don't get to use this every time we disagree. She can't go around breaking laws and get away with things just because she knows you."

"Fine." Jenna crossed her arms and glared at him.

He glared back.

I considered a quick escape that didn't involve trying to use the oversize moving van as a getaway vehicle. These older streets were too narrow. I'd never make the first corner at high speed.

"Max? What the hell?"

Ben stood at the bottom of the stoop's steps, hands raised to his sides as if to echo the question, glaring at Officer Darby.

"I was joking."

"You've got one panicked and the other one looking like she's going to murder you and hide the body somewhere only the most devious minds would find. And if you don't think she could do it, you haven't read her latest book."

"I'm sorry." Officer Darby sounded beyond exasperated, which would have been...Huh, what's beyond exasperated?

Ben kept that steady look focused on Max and nodded his head in my direction.

Max took a step toward me, waving his hand around as if he didn't know what to do with it. Then stepped back. "Ms. Lane...Kasey. I'm sorry. Let's just leave it at that."

I could tell he didn't want to, that part of him really was annoyed that I'd done damage and was just going to get away with it. Except for the fact that now that I lived here, I'd probably be outside every morning checking on the tree's healing process.

He glanced around, desperate to find something. Who knows what mental rope guys look to grab onto in situations like this.

But, as apologies went, it didn't stink as much as it could have. Even with the fadeout.

"That's okay." I said, trying hard to mean it.

"Max, why don't you go upstairs and carry down whatever box is the heaviest." Ben glared at his friend until Max headed toward the front door, giving him a hard shove as he headed inside. "Max can be..."

Now that Ben had taken over the reprimand, Jenna was looking her perky self again. "Max is a great guy. Don't worry. He won't be a you-know-what again."

It wasn't so much the you-know-what'ness of his words. It was that this was just one more thing.

I was supposed to be embracing my newfound freedom, finding the way to build a better life for myself. This was my chance to grow on my own, to spread my wings. I felt like one of those stupid kids who didn't know how to do her own laundry or make her bed at college because she'd never had to do anything on her own.

I was a decision-making virgin.

I'd let life and Jason pull me along until I felt like all my options were gone.

The idea that Officer Darby was there at every one of my failures for the last forty-eight hours, that he redirected each of my disasters, grated. Like cheap parmesan over an expensive, handmade pasta. And I still had to deal with today's disaster.

"What about the tree?" Yeah, look at me taking charge.

Ben came around and looked at it, pressing the bark back into place.

"No real damage. You dinged it, but didn't take off enough bark to hurt the tree in the long run. Why don't you give me the keys and I'll park the van while you guys bring the first load up?"

That was an offer I wasn't going to refuse. Learning to make my own way in the world was one thing. Knowing when to let someone more capable do what I wanted done anyway was completely another.

I was willing to be all Independent Woman except when parking. I really hated parking.

Jenna and I each grabbed a box and headed toward the stairs.

"Really, Kasey." Jenna waited to let me pass into the foyer. She already had her game face on. Who knew where this was going. "Max is a good guy. He has a big sense of humor. He probably feels horrible about making you feel bad."

Not as bad as I felt. I was one step away from a tree murderer. I was a tree maimer.

"Hey." Max stood at the top of the stairs, his arms wrapped around a box.

"Hey." I watched tiny Jenna slide by him then went to do the same. And of course, not-quite-as-tiny me practically knocked the box out of his hands while juggling to hold onto my own. "Sorry. I didn't mean to…"

"Don't worry about it." He juggled the box until he could brace it on top of the banister. I tried to read his expression behind his mirrored Ray-Bans. "Listen, I get it. You're having a crappy week. Ben called me and gave me an earful in the four minutes I've been upstairs. You seem to be managing a lot right now."

"Well, I'll admit, watching you handle Jason was fun."

"Handling Jason *was* fun." He grinned and a dimple kicked in. Just on the one side. The right, where his mouth hitched up the slightest bit—not quite crooked.

"So, yeah." I dragged my gaze away from that dimple. He probably used it to hypnotize female perps into submission. Do cops actually say *perps*? Anyway…"Let's just call it good and get the moving done."

I pushed past him, trying to ignore the dimple. I was not looking for a guy and if I was, Officer Max Darby was as far from the polished, soft-spoken guy I was going to look for next. After Jason, I knew I wanted someone who treated me as an equal and respected my worth. Someone who didn't scream Command and Control while standing still.

When my life was up and running, I'd look for a guy who fit in it with me. But, until then, no men. Not even just a flirt. I was looking to start my new business and steer clear of domineering men.

I glanced at Max's shoulders as he carried the box down the stairs and tried to justify that looking from afar couldn't do any harm.

Far, far afar.

ELEVEN

I AVOIDED MAX as much as possible for the rest of the day. That didn't mean I wasn't aware of him. It was nearly impossible not to be. As the day got warmer, he and Ben stripped off their jackets and toted heavy things around like they were feathers. There was much eye-candy to be had.

Eye-candy was acceptable. I mean, they say that a large number of serial killers are gorgeous, but I'd avoid them too.

Too bad it wasn't July. Although, in this the neighborhood. I doubted even that heat level would have gotten them out of the t-shirts they were dusting up.

I wasn't sure what it was about Max that had my attention. He was shorter than Ben, probably five-ten, maybe five-eleven. And, while he was darkly handsome, standing next to Ben's golden good-looks, he had abrupt edges that seemed at odds with his charm.

But, there was something that had my gaze returning to him again and again.

Maybe it was that he'd been my unintentional hero over the last twenty-four hours, calling off ex-boyfriends and snotty landlords.

"He's single."

"What?" I tried to pretend I was looking out the window behind where the guys were dissembling Ben's bed.

"Max. He's single."

This was the last thing I needed. Jenna seemed like one of those *I'm happy as a couple so everyone else must be happy as well* people.

"Yeah." How to say this nicely? "I'm not really in a looking-to-date place right now."

"Sure." Jenna was so cute trying to look innocent that it was hard to be annoyed with her.

"Seriously. You've heard about my past couple days. The last thing I need is a guy. Actually, the last thing I *want* is a guy. I really don't need some guy mucking up my life reboot."

"Sure," she said again.

I believed her even less.

"I'm moving into the *I Am Woman, Hear Me Roar* part of my life."

Jenna nodded.

"Plus, he's completely not my type."

Jenna slid her gaze toward the guys, dragging mine along with it just as Max tugged the bottom of his t-shirt up and ducked to wipe his forehead, showing off an impressive six pack.

"Right." I cleared my throat. "But, I know what I'm looking for and he's not it. When I start looking I'm going to meet a guy I have things in common with. Who is going to see me as an equal." Not the punch line of a joke.

"His last girlfriend was *horrible*."

"Seriously, Jenna."

"Actually, she was worse than horrible. She was like rom com evil villainess evil."

I put down the box I'd been moving to the kitchen figuring I might as well just wait her out.

"He volunteers with kids. He coaches baseball."

I glanced at the rag in my hand considering gagging her.

"His family is from Chicago and he flies home for every major holiday. But he still says this is home."

"Don't care."

"He saved a kitten last week."

"A kitten?" Okay. So that got my attention. What kind of guy actually rescues kittens?

"Yup. Climbed right up the tree and carried her down to her seven-year-old owner."

"You're making that up."

"Nope. He's totally embarrassed by it. Hold on." She pulled her phone out and shuffled through some pages. "It made the local Patch."

Yup. There was Max, a seven-year-old girl looking at him like he was a super hero, holding a kitten and looking like he'd like to be anywhere else.

"Huh. He saved a kitten."

"They're not letting him live it down at work."

"Well, why would they?" If police departments were anything like Law & Order had taught me, there would be kitten posters all over the place by the end of the week. "But still."

Jenna gave me her own version of The Look.

"Okay." She grabbed a box to carry down with her. "This last guy must have been quite a prize."

"It's more that I hadn't realized what a prize he was." I did a mental rundown of everything I must have missed again, cataloging things that may or may not have been clues to Jason's jerkiness. "Plus, twenty-four hours is not enough time to recover, rebuild, and move on."

And that was just my ego I was talking about. Who knew if that was more or less resilient than a heart? Luckily, I wasn't going to have to find out since my heart had recovered before I'd even made it to the curb.

"You can't blame yourself for trusting someone in your inner circle. And no one should be more inner circle than your long-term boyfriend."

"It's just—"

"I know. The dumping. The half-security deposit. The general idiotness."

"You have no idea."

Jenna gave me what I'm sure she thought was a reassuring smile but just made me want to ask her what she was up to. Before I could double down on my warning, she turned back to the box she was taping up.

We worked all morning getting Ben's basics packed and moved to Jenna's. Things like his bed and books we wrapped up and put in the small storage area in the attic. Everything else was staying right where it was. Which was perfect all around.

The entire time, Jenna kept smiling to herself.

You can't blame me for keeping an eye on her after that. Any sane woman would have.

~~*~~

When everything was packed or stored, we headed down the street to a pizza place Ben swore by. He'd even pointed out the magnet on the fridge and suggested I memorize the number.

It was nice to have some sure things in place. I pulled out my credit card, planning to pay for everyone as a thank you.

"You don't have to do that." Jenna slid it back across the counter toward me.

"Yes I do. I want to say thanks for the help and the place to stay and everything you guys have done." It was embarrassing to admit, but..."Most of my friends are still back in Ohio. I'd been so busy when I moved here that I didn't really go out and meet the kind of friends who you call when you move. I met Jason and got serious with him pretty quickly when I got here for grad school. Life just stayed really focused."

Or, *narrow* more likely.

They all just stared at me. I could tell the guys were embarrassed. Jenna just did that grinning thing. She had to be the happiest person I'd ever met.

"I know exactly what you mean. I just fired one of my best friends. The other one is a writer who lives on the other side of town. And everyone else I'm close with is back home. I followed my boyfriend to college where he basically dumped me the day before our wedding."

"Wow. You're making my story look lame."

"I'm here to help." She said it in her standard pixie-cute way making me believe she actually was sharing to help.

"But, I really would like to buy the thank you meal. We've all had a big week. I started a new company, Jenna has Ben moved in, and Ben has someone to sublet his place."

Max toasted all of us with his drink then asked, "What about me?"

It was too easy. And I stilled owed him for scaring me about the accident. "Oh, you've had the biggest week of all."

"I have?"

"You're a hero. I saw you on the front page. Rescuer of Kittens!"

Max set his drink down and glared at Jenna. "Jenna."

"What?" She turned her phone on where she had just made it the background, and flashed the group. "It's adorable."

"If I'd been carrying a pregnant woman out of an exploding building, that's the kind of pictures you show. Kittens. No, Jenna. Don't show that to anyone else."

"But..." I could see this was going somewhere Max wasn't going to like.

"What did you do?"

"Nothing *too* big."

"Jenna." Max actually sounded a little threatening.

Jenna glanced toward Ben as if he was going to take care of this.

"Don't look at me, Sunshine. I'm guessing what you did and you know we have rules about that."

Max all but gasped. "You didn't."

"You never said I couldn't. Ben told you about the rules and you called him a chicken. But, you know, a worse word."

I was trying to figure out what was going on between the gasping and allusions and self-censorship.

"This is true." Ben gave him one of those completely unapologetic shrugs friends do when they really have nothing else to say. "This is what you get for questioning my manhood."

"Your manhood is coming up a lot today," I said, not really sure what we were talking about.

"It's true." Ben took a swig of his beer and grinned. "Still comfortable. Also, ignoring the non-mixed company joke potential in that statement."

"Jenna?" Max prompted.

"Yes. It's on my website. It's already become a meme. My teens have started captioning it and passing it on. I wouldn't suggest checking out #OfficerMax today on Twitter."

Oh. My. Gosh.

Did Jenna have a death wish?

If she did, she was working overtime on it. She pulled out her phone and called up Twitter. "Here's a few of my favorites."

Max snatched the phone and paged through, horrified noises coming out of his mouth as he clicked one link after another.

"Hug me, I'm a cop? I'd climb a tree for that too? Officer Max can—" Max's eyes widened and he set the phone face down on the table. "I'm not sure your audience is strictly teens at this point. Jenna, how could you?"

"But, Officer Max, you said nothing I could put on my website that was true would embarrass you. You said Ben was being a *pansy* for not letting me post pictures of him."

"I didn't think you'd do this!"

"It's not like it isn't already in the newspaper."

Max stabbed a finger toward the phone. "Officer Max, Seducer of Kittens? That's just wrong, Jenna. Just plain wrong."

"I bet you're wishing you were in on the rules now." Ben leaned back, angling toward Jenna, and slid an arm over the back of her chair

"Whatever these rules are, I want in on them now." I glanced toward the phone afraid of what would happen if the Underwear Situation was online as I tried to build my brand. That would be quite a brand all right. "I want it retroactive back to when we met as I wasn't offered the deal ahead of time."

"I want what she said." Max crossed his arms, the glaring spread out now to all three of us.

"So, no more #OfficerMax tweets?" Jenna actually looked upset. "What will I tell the Camisoles?"

I glanced at Ben, already aware he was an expert Jenna Interpreter.

"Her fan group," he answered under their argument.

"You'll come up with something."

"But, Max. They love you. I have people who have read my books just because of you. When you were one of the cops who went to speak about gun violence in schools to worried parents after the scare three towns over, people donated to those families all week."

I could see Max's inner battle in his expression—no dimple in sight. Of course he was the type of guy who wanted to do good things. That's why he was a cop. But he also didn't like becoming one of Jenna's characters. I was betting the Officer Max tweets were even larger than life than anything Max could stumble into.

There were probably t-shirts and fangirl sites. I needed to Google this immediately. I glanced toward my bag wondering if I could pull out my phone without adding to the table tension.

This was seriously the best meal ever.

And, thank goodness I'd retroactively invoked my privacy rights.

"Jenna, I'll make you a deal. We'll let Kasey decide." He smiled at me, obviously trying to win me over with his charm. Trying to convince me to vote pro-Max. "As a matter of fact, I went out on a really interesting call last night. A landlord situation—"

"Down with Officer Max!" I pumped my fist in the air. "You totally don't need those stories. Friendship is far too important! And, Twitter is so 2009."

Everyone was looking at me like I'd lost my mind.

"I'm just saying," I continued. "Maybe Max doesn't like his exploits blasted over the internet."

"Obviously." Max cocked an eyebrow at me.

"And, I'm sure the police department doesn't want him becoming some internet poster boy."

"This is a good point." The cocky grin was back.

"And what about the innocents? Those poor people Officer Max rescues who don't want their story going international with a bunch of teenage girls?"

"I don't know." Max tapped his chin as if thinking that one over. "The one last night was pretty good. She didn't even know what day it was."

"I'm sure she knew what day it was."

"We almost had an indecent exposure situation on our hands."

"I doubt that's what happened."

"Oh, it was close."

"I'm sure the poor, innocent, covered girl knew what day it was and—"

Jenna had set down her Diet Coke and was watching us like a tennis match on crack. "This sounds even more dangerous than the kitten situation."

Max nodded. "This culprit had sharper claws."

Now he was just out of line. "How would you know?"

"Excuse me." Jenna leaned forward. "Could you guys slow down a bit?"

That's when I noticed she'd pulled out a little red notebook again. Ben shook his head like he knew what was going to happen next.

"Max," Jenna tapped her pen against her chin. "Did you arrest Kasey last night?"

"If I arrested Kasey, would she have been here bright and early to assault another inanimate object?"

I kicked him under the table. "Oh look. A third inanimate object I attacked this week."

"Is there something you two would like to tell us?" Jenna smiled what I'm sure she thought was a reassuring smile, but I saw the evil pixie gleam underneath.

I eyed the notebook. I eyed Jenna's smile. "No."

"Well, actually—"

I kicked Max under the table again.

"—No."

"Max, I'll give you twenty dollars to tell me what's going on."

Ben laughed. "Twenty dollars is a lot for Jenna."

"Don't." I warned under my breath.

Max gave me this look that told me I was in a lot of trouble. "I told you to behave."

"I was behaving. That wasn't my fault."

"What wasn't?" Jenna prompted, her pen leaving an inky dot across her page.

I watched him make the decision, watched him fold it back up in his head and put it away.

"I'm afraid I'm not allowed to disclose some of what goes on at work."

It was silly, but I was thankful. Jenna was the first girl I really felt I could be friends with since moving here. I'd had classmates in grad school I Facebooked with. You know, the people you studied with, but outside of class everyone was so busy with work and family and keeping it together that you didn't hang out. At work, I stepped into a manager role right away and had to keep a bit of distance from the other people in their twenties because a bunch of them reported to me.

But, glancing at Jenna and the life she had, I could see myself trying to wedge my way into their merry little band.

You know, if they didn't decide I was certifiably insane first.

Just as I was trying to come up with the next topic of conversation to get things moving as quickly as possible away from my bare-butted breaking-and-entering situation, the pizza showed up.

Thank goodness for small favors.

With the food came some type of ongoing toppings argument I could barely follow until we were down to the last slice.

"Ben, are you going to need the van again today?" I dipped my pizza crust in ranch dressing as they all looked at me funny.

I wasn't going to defend myself. It was good and that's all the excuse I needed.

"No. Next weekend I'll have to come by and do some more packing. But I think we got enough out of your way that you can start to settle in, right?"

"Definitely." I was in awe. He'd even cleaned. I'd been able to smell the bleach when I'd gotten there that morning. "So, I'll drop you guys all back at Ben's, get my stuff from Jason's, and return the van if no one else needs to move anything."

"Wait." Jenna set her pizza down. I'd already learned when she wanted to discuss something she got rid of whatever was in her hands. "You have to go to that guy's place?"

"Most of my stuff was already there."

"How much stuff?"

Fortunately—or unfortunately, depending on how you looked at it—not much since Craigslist had snatched up most of my belongings.

"Only five boxes."

"All your clothes fit in five boxes?"

"Well, plus one box of shoes, some books, and don't forget the two suitcases we moved today. But yeah, that's about it."

"I'll go with you." Jenna's hands had fisted on the table. I almost wanted to see what it was like to set a hundred pounds of rage loose on someone. The whole world probably underestimated the Power of the Pixie.

"You don't have to do that." Part of me really wanted her nowhere near this. To not meet Jason and see what an idiot I was. One of them had already seen that in action. The other part did not want to go alone.

"Oh, I'm coming. That's what friends are for." She picked up her pizza. Obviously, that was the end of the discussion.

"I'm coming too." Ben shrugged. "Someone has to move the boxes. Plus, if Jenna's going to go on the offensive, someone's gotta move Jenna."

"Hey. You know how I feel about bullies."

Ben leaned over and kissed her on the forehead. "That's why I said I'd go too. Not that I didn't think you should go."

"Great." Max tossed his napkin on his plate and stood. "One more stop and we're done for the day."

I watched him head toward the men's room while Ben and Jenna discussed where they were going to put all Ben's clothes they couldn't store for the next three weeks.

Somehow, without even noticing it, I'd gotten a posse— and a pretty rocking one at that.

Life was looking up.

TWELVE

WE PULLED UP TO the curb and parked the van in a commercial loading zone.

"I'll wait here in case a cop comes by." Max slid the side door open and hopped out. "It's probably best if I stay out of sight. Who knows what that idiot will accuse you of if you show up with me in tow?"

Oh. I hadn't thought of that. But, it was probably true. I could see another 911 call in our future if Jason saw Max. He'd probably call in a counter-terrorist group on a conspiracy report.

We rang and went through the whole who-is-it-it's-me thing and a long pause before Jason finally rang us up. He probably didn't know if he wanted my stuff out more than he didn't want to deal with me.

His building—the one that had seemed so clean and modern just three days ago—felt sterile and ugly now. The warm charm of Jenna's world had ruined me forever.

I'd expected Jason to be waiting at the door, my boxes there and ready to go. But when we got to his floor, the door was shut. With an internal eye-roll at the power play, I slid the key he'd given me into the lock and turned.

Or attempted to turn it.

He'd managed to change the locks in the seventyish hours since our fond farewell. Heck, he'd probably had it done before we even had dinner.

What did he think? I was going to copy the key and break in and steal his hidden collection of weird Hallmark cards?

Maybe.

Orrr not.

I pounded on the door, counted to thirty, and pounded again.

"I'm not really seeing the draw yet." Ben said under his breath before Jenna smacked him in the gut.

One door down on the opposite side opened.

Great.

"Hi Mrs. Gershwin. How are you?"

"What's all the racket you're making? Kasey Lane, why are you pounding on that door?"

"Sorry, Mrs. Gershwin. I'm just here to pick up my stuff."

Her gaze moved from me to Jenna and Ben and back. "Finally left the jerk, did ya? Can't say I'm surprised. Should have done it forever ago. No good that one. All selfishness. Why don't you just let yourself in? I'll come down if you need someone to witness you don't take anything that isn't yours."

"Well, he's in there. But, he's changed the lock."

"In my day, a man wouldn't have changed the lock on his woman unless she was bringing home something besides the groceries. You can do better. Is this one single?" She pointed a shaky finger at Ben.

"Nope. He's taken by the very dangerous pixie behind me. Definitely not a woman to cross."

"Those are the best kind." She stepped back toward her door, sticking a foot out to keep her Yorkie inside. "Good to have at your back. Well, you take care kiddo."

Her door closed behind her with a solid thud, the sound of her TV blaring turned back up.

"That's the nicest that woman has ever been to me."

"Really? She seemed to like you."

Or was just really glad to see me gone.

"So, what do you think we should do?"

It had to have been five minutes since we'd rung the bell and been let inside. Jason knew we were just standing out in his hall. He probably thought I was alone and getting frustrated and upset. It was definitely a power move.

It was time to shove every piece of assumption down his throat. I bet the door would open pretty darn quickly then.

There were two things Jason hated, and he'd already had one this week because of me.

"Laugh."

"What?"

"Laugh. Loud. Like we're joking around and I'm telling you the funniest story you've ever heard. And it's about Jason."

He hated a scene—unless, of course, it was in defense of his car—and he hated not knowing what was going on.

Jenna started up, laughing like an insane person which actually got Ben laughing for real. Then Jenna started laughing because Ben was laughing at her which got *me* laughing. Then, I don't know if I could have stopped if someone held a gun to my head. It was all so absurd.

The door cracked open and we all fell silent like it had been a cue. But, when I saw Jason standing there torn between annoyance, smugness, and blatant curiosity, I started giggling. Followed by Jenna's little snort. Followed by Ben covering his mouth and turning to look down the hall.

"What?" Jason covered his curiosity with his typical arrogant demeanor.

"Nothing. We were just chatting about..." I let it hang out there as if I hadn't been able to make up a lie. Which was true, but not for the reason he thought. "The building."

"So?"

"So what?"

"What about the building?"

"Oh." I glanced at my dynamic duo and then back. "Well, it's just my new place is a lot cuter. But, you were never a cutesy kind of person, so this is probably perfect for you."

He stared me down as if there was something I wasn't telling him. There was a lot I wasn't telling him, but none of it was his business.

"So, I wanted to pick up my stuff."

You'd think I'd just said I'd like to steal all your belongings the way he looked at me.

"You know," I continued. "The boxes we'd brought over last weekend."

"Right. Fine." Jason pushed the door open.

I headed in, expecting again to find them neatly stacked by the door. That would have made too much sense.

"Where is everything?"

Jason waved a hand in the general direction of the bedroom. "Wherever you put it."

I'd had enough. It wasn't funny anymore and I didn't see any reason for small talk. I brushed past him, aware of Jenna and Ben following close behind, and picked up the first box. Of course it was books. Ben took it from me before I managed to tip myself backward and get trapped under it.

"Why don't we just carry everything out to the hall then make a couple trips?"

Jenna's arms were crossed as she glared at Jason leaning against the bedroom door's frame. "Are you sure?"

I glanced at Jason again. "Yup. I just want to get out of here."

He gave me that smirk—the one I'd been mistaking for a smile for the last few years. In that moment I was sure it wasn't that I needed to get away from him. It wasn't that my heart was so broken that this was killing me. It was that I'd just realized how *annoying* he was, and really, why put up with that when you can just leave?

We moved all the boxes while Jason watched, probably making sure we didn't lift anything from his room. With three of us and five boxes it wasn't such a bad trip. Ben and I went back for the last two while Jenna paced out front giving Max the rundown of what an idiot I'd dated.

And maybe what an idiot I'd had to have been to date him.

When we'd put everything in the van, I slammed the door with a happy expectation of never seeing Jason again.

"So, did you flatten anything while you were up there? Did he have an air mattress or something you could unplug the nozzle on?"

88

Even Ben just looked at him like he was an idiot.

But, at least this idiot wasn't mine to deal with.

And, as we pulled from the curb, I had to admit, not even a little part of me felt sad as I watched the address I'd planned to call home disappear down the street behind us.

THIRTEEN

I WAS LYING IN bed, listening to the peaceful sounds of a neighborhood that didn't abut the highway, when my phone rang.

I was shockingly unsurprised to see it was Jenna.

"Just wanted to make sure you were okay and had everything you needed."

Of course she did. I'm not sure what she would have done if I said I didn't have something, but it was nice to be checked on.

"Yup. All set." I stretched and glanced out the window at new leaves shifting to yellow-orange on the trees hiding the building behind us. "This is the most relaxed I've been in…years."

I thought back trying to remember the last time I truly felt at ease and couldn't remember a better time than tonight.

"Great. Just, you know…checking we didn't scare you off." Jenna gave a little laugh as if she were joking, but I could hear the nerves behind it.

It hadn't dawned on me that she was serious about trying to find girlfriends. And, with Ben leaving, she was kind of in the same boat...not really, but the end result was still her guy would be gone. Of course he wasn't a controlling, manipulative, cruel SOB. She was apparently way smarter about this guy thing than I was.

"Nope. Not scared off. Maybe a bit nervous'ed off at first, but hey. You guys seem relatively harmless."

"Well, you haven't met Dane yet." She gave a little laugh, wished me good night, and hung up.

This Dane guy must be something else...and *still* off limits.

Mental Note: No matter how hot Dane is, stay far, far away. Think hoopskirts.

~~*~~

Last night I dreamt of Max Darby.

That was truly the last thing I wanted. I didn't want to be waking up with a smile on my face thinking about the way he handled tough situations with humor, or the deep dimple that sinks into his right cheek each time he smiles, or the fact that he knew how to maneuver around Jenna's quirks...or him and kittens, darn it.

The entire dream was about tons of calendars of stupid Officer Darby holding kittens.

White kittens. Grey kittens. Sleek kittens. Fluffy kittens. Kittens in little police hats.

It was absurd.

Okay, Subconscious. I get it. He's a good guy.

But, not for me. I was not going to fall for a guy like Max Darby. I wanted security and routine and similar tastes and values and hobbies.

I did not want a cocky cop who seemed to thrive on mocking me.

So, Subconscious, stick that in your vault and throw away the key. I had a plan to succeed as an independent woman and no guy, no matter how flat his stomach or how deep his dimple, was going to run this train off the tracks.

~~*~~

So, this was going to be fun.

Not.

"Hello?" My mom's high, stilted voice came over the phone. She was one of those people who even with a cell phone I'd programmed with my name and picture still acted like she didn't know who was on the other end when she picked up.

"Hi, Mom. It's me." I closed my eyes thinking about the last few days and followed up with, "Kasey."

You know—in case she didn't know *me* was her only daughter.

"Kasey. This is a nice surprise."

That's not a bad start.

Now I just have to break it to her that the guy she thought was perfect, was...not so much.

My mom and the male gender as a whole were on some very rocky ground. Their relationship had turned a bit sour a few years ago. Ok, a few decades ago. Things were rolling along just fine, my mom not being bitter at all—or so she said—about giving up her potential career as a backup singer to be a wife and mother.

When I was six, having a perfectly good day in kindergarten (it was my turn to get pushed on the swings and I'd just gotten an underdog so high my shoe flew off) my mom showed up at the school, damp tissue in one hand, the letter from my dad in the other, and dragged me home to explain that I was now fatherless.

The problem wasn't so much that he left, since he hadn't been around a lot as far as my younger self could remember. The problem was more my mother's perceived reasons for him leaving.

My dad was a company man. He'd seen my mother at a club, told her she was pretty and smelled like spring flowers and chased her until she said yes.

I've heard the tale of their marriage more than most girls have heard Cinderella. Beautiful, young, up-and-coming singer marries beneath her only to find out that two worlds colliding don't make sparks, they just implode. Aged beauty is left on her own to raise daughter while teaching her to never make the same mistakes she made when she herself was but a lass.

The end.

Yup. For my mom, that is literally the end. There's no more grand adventures or a chance to go back to school or a new job. She's just going to stay the personal aid to Mrs. Ferske and avoid all men for the rest of her life.

Shockingly enough, she loved Jason.

Proof that while bitterness isn't hereditary, maybe bad decision making is.

"I hope I'm catching you at a good time." I really, really hope so.

"Yup. I'm just about to reorganize the tax files, but…" Mom's voice drifted off as if she dropped the phone and doesn't realize it.

This could go on for a bit, so I brush my teeth. Might as well fill that part of the morning with good hygiene.

"Sorry about that. I'm back. I was trying to use that ear thing. Mrs. Ferske likes to call me when I'm driving, but this thing never works. Anyway, how are things with you?"

"Well, I have some news about work. And about Jason."

Loaded silence and then, "Oh?"

"It's just, there've been some changes at work and they're going to impact my relationship with Jason, and—"

"Is your office moving you? Did you get another promotion? I am *so* proud of you."

"No. No, actually…" I bit my lip, hard. Trying to break this to her. All she ever wanted was for me to have a successful career in a glamorous field. When *Mad Men* came on the air, she all but applied to grad school for me. In retrospect, Jason was probably a power-couple accessory in her mind. "*Actually*, there were some things going on at the office and it opened a new door for me,"—Yeah. The exit—"and because of this new opportunity I've been able to head out on my own."

"You mean, you're working at your own branch?"

"No. I mean I had the chance to start my own company. I actually met with my first client yesterday,"—If Jenna really does hire me—"and I'm excited about the work we'll be doing together."

"Your own business?" The way her voice went up at the end told me just how excited she was. I didn't need to hear her clapping her hands together to know. "Oh, Kasey. This is so exciting. You're a *business owner.* I can't believe it. Wait until Pam hears this. Her daughter, Joy, just built a school in the Congo and she thinks that's just such a big deal."

Um...

"But, she'll *never* own her own business while she's running around the globe building things for other people. It's not as if a school is saving lives."

I have learned when to just keep my mouth shut.

"What does Jason think of this?" she asked.

"Well..." If I was bending the truth, I might as well stretch it as well. "Jason and I couldn't really agree on what we wanted. It's not that he didn't want me to start the business. But he definitely liked how things were and wasn't looking for any type of big change."

Yeah. Not bad. Basically all true.

"But, didn't you move in with him this week?" The suspicion was starting to creep back into her voice. "You're not telling me everything, are you?"

"No." I tried to keep the lying to a minimum. But at the same time, I knew anything I said about Jason was just going to feed the Men As Disrupters of Happiness fire. "So, Jason...the thing is, when I told him I had big news, I kind of expected him to be happy. I mean, I know it was going to be a huge adjustment, but couples go through this every day. I thought we'd be fine. I thought he was ready for this."

And, I had. I really hadn't even worried about my change in employment status being a deal breaker.

Talk about blindsided.

"Oh my word. You're pregnant. Oh dear, sweet, lord Jesus. I knew it. I knew you'd end up pregnant and not married and he's going to be thinking now about how maybe he doesn't want to get married. Maybe he doesn't want a baby. Sweetheart, you can move home. Actually, you should move home. You can just do all that work for your new business remotely, right? Everything's online now. Just the other day Pam showed me how she was talking to her daughter all the way across the ocean on that new thing...Skype, have you heard of it? It's just the darndest thing. You could work like that. And then we could raise your daughter here. Oh, that could be fun. A little baby. I can paint the back room pink. Or maybe yellow. I read that girls don't like pink any more. What do you think?"

All five stages of grief and I hadn't even told her what was wrong yet. My mom, the optimist.

Great to see all that faith she had in my relationship.

"On the upside, I'm definitely not pregnant." So no need to move home. Small blessings. "But, Jason and I broke up."

"Because of your new company."

My new company.

"Kind of. He didn't like the idea that I wasn't working for a corporation anymore. The lack of stability really bothered him and he thought we weren't...you know...equals any more."

I closed my eyes and rested my head back against the bed. Had we ever been equals? Had Jason always seen me as the student? The girl he helped teach and took under his wing and walked through the hiring process. Even now, a few years later, running my own department for a multi-million dollar company, did he see me still as the kid he slept with?

That sounded totally different in my head than I meant it.

"Well, then, don't you worry about that honey." My mom sucked in a deep breath and let it out.

I waited for the anti-man rampage, but instead she said, "You'll just find someone more worthy of you."

I glanced at the calendar…nothing about Hell or ice or pigs or anything. Maybe I should consider not leaving the house today.

FOURTEEN

S O, YOU FINALLY LEFT the jackass."

"Jayne?" This was exactly who I needed. I just
hadn't known it until I heard her voice on the other
end of the line. "Have you been talking to my mother?"

As if. Jayne had been the voice of reason to my mother's
man-hating ways since we met in Driver's Ed. The chances of
Jayne hanging out with my mom were up there with a cozy
dinner between all the Middle East leaders.

"Yeah. Right. Barbara and I have been having tea and
knitting scarves for the homeless every Sunday."

"It's still a little too warm for tea and scarves."

"A little too pleasant to ruin it with *quality* time with
Barbara."

Well, there was that too.

"So, how'd you hear about Jason?"

"You obviously haven't looked at Facebook recently."

"I've been a little busy."

Understatement.

"Jason has a nice little smear campaign going on."

I was already firing up my computer before she even got to *smear*.

Pictures of his car in the parking lot—rims on the ground. Pictures of his wine stained sweater. Pictures of my boxes piled in his bedroom. Complaints about my attitude. And one really long post about how I'd gotten fired.

Unbelievable.

"I was under the impression that he was smart enough to know what libel was." Apparently everything I'd thought about him was wrong.

His name probably wasn't even Jason.

"So you haven't broken up?"

"Oh, we have definitely broken up." I scrolled through his page amazed the only thing he had to post was about us-past-tense. And I thought *I* needed a life. "We *so* have."

"But you didn't pour wine on him or slash his tires?"

"I totally did those things too." I reran the night through my head, enjoying the wine thing especially. "Actually, I didn't slash his tires. I just let the air out of them. I highly recommend it as a stress reliever."

"And you were fired?" Leave it to Jayne to get back to the important point that quickly.

"Not really. I got laid off. They got rid of a bunch of the first level managers so, there I went."

I still wasn't over the fact that they thought an upper management person could take on all my people, accounts, and workload when no one could even tell you what they did except for dress nice and play golf. But, that wasn't my problem anymore, was it?

"And?" she pushed.

I ran Jayne through the entire time from losing my job through my breakup with Jason to meeting Jenna at the Brew Ha Ha and moving into Ben's before I mentioned as casually as possible starting my own business.

When I finished, Jayne was still laughing at me.

And this was my support system.

"Kasey, why didn't you call me?" Instead of being annoyed, she just sounded exasperated.

That was part of the entire problem. I'd let my world narrow to my job and Jason and whatever Jason thought our world should look like. Not only was I completely embarrassed by this, but I felt guilty. So guilty. I was that girl. The one who disappeared because of a guy.

"I felt like I didn't have the right to call you just because I'd hit a rough patch."

For once I didn't know what the silence on the other end of the line meant. Maybe this is where she told me I was right, I didn't have the right to call her, to lean on her just because things had gotten rough and I had no where else to turn.

"So…" I dragged it out, knowing I owed her an apology and realizing how amazingly lucky I was to have a friend who came to the rescue without even a mayday call being made. "I felt horrible. I hadn't realized how insular I'd become until I was sitting in The Brew realizing I had no one to call to come get me. No one to go out and get chocolate cake and cheap wine drunk. I'd let Jason take over. How was I supposed to just turn around and be like, *Oh, Jayne, I need you?*"

I heard Jayne let out a deep sigh. Whatever it was, I definitely deserved it.

"Kasey, we're not those girls."

"I kn—"

"No. I don't mean we're not the girls who get lost along the way. I mean, we are not and we will never be those girls who can't forgive each other."

"But this is a mistake that lasted years."

"If I believed in karma, I'd say you prepaid this mistake by dealing with Jason all that time." The swoosh of Jayne sucking in a breath on the other end filled my ear. "I never liked him. I never liked how he talked to you. When I came to visit, you were already so serious and anything he said you'd jump to make happen. You changed your look and your plans. If I'd been there, if I'd done a better job at staying in touch when I started school, I might have been able to nudge you away from him. But, I was so involved in my own drama that I didn't even notice he was controlling you to such an extent. Then, I was afraid if I rocked the boat I'd lose you completely."

I let my eyes drop shut, surprised at the venom in Jayne's voice.

"Kasey?"

"Yeah." It was my turn to suck in a breath. I didn't want her to think things were always horrible. "You're right about how I let him treat me. He was…controlling. And I should have seen through that sooner. But, I'm not your responsibility."

I was no one's responsibility and that's how it was going to stay.

"Maybe not." Jayne gave in that much, but stayed firm. "But, I feel like I didn't have your back when you needed it."

"We're both here now and we're not going to let bad decisions damage our awesomeness again." I prayed that was true. That she'd forgive me even as I fought to forgive myself.

"Cheers to that! So…tell me about these new friends you're making and if I'm going to have to fly out there to clear them this time."

I rushed through descriptions, letting her know about Jenna and Ben. About hitting the tree and Max showing up. About how Max had been the cop who had already almost arrested me twice. I told her about the apartment and the move and getting pizza. As the words came out, I realized I needed to say them as much as she needed to hear them. That I needed to hear how well things were going too.

"Holy cow, Kasey. You have to get with this cop."

Okay, so…that was adamant. And out of the blue.

"Um, no. I just told you he'd just be another man telling me what to do. He'd make Jason look like a push-over. Jason mentored me right into a trophy girlfriend. I was pretty enough, and smart enough, and I had the right job title and I fit in his life. I understood things we enjoyed like the symphony and jazz and—"

"Do you even like the symphony?" Jayne's voice dripped with more doubt than would fit in a bathtub.

"Well, sometimes. I mean, some of it's really great."

"But, let's say, we're driving in your car—"

"I don't have a car."

"In the real world you'd have a car. And, we're driving in it. And the top's down—"

"My imaginary car is a convertible? I'm doing pretty darn well in this new reality."

"*As I was saying,* the top's down and the sun is shining and we're about to go shopping—"

"Since apparently I'm rich."

"—and you reach for the radio to turn on the CD you put in just for the drive. Don't think about it. Quick, what comes on?"

"Kesha." Wait, what?

"Really? Kesha?"

"Well, we're going shopping and the top's down, so Kesha."

"Do you even own a Kesha CD?" Jayne sounded more shocked by that than anything I'd told her so far.

"No. But, I'm downloading one right now." I pulled the phone from my ear, hearing Jayne's voice drift away. "Hold on, she has a couple. What's the one with her when she dressed nuts? Oh. Here it is."

I hit the purchase button and raised the phone back to my ear.

"I now own a Kesha CD for when we take my convertible downtown to go shopping."

"Okay, so this is a step in the right direction." Jayne sighed and I'm pretty sure she's mumbling the word *Kesha* under her breath. "My point really wasn't to go buy some drunk, party girl music. It was more the fact that you were fitting yourself into Jason's life. You aren't even sure who you are right now. You can't blame all that on Jason."

Ouch.

"Jayne, you're making my argument for me. I need to stay far, far away from all men right now. *Especially* men who like to be in control." I glanced around for something cheerful to focus on. "Betas are underrated. I need to find a nice guy who I enjoy but doesn't need to be in charge of everything.

Someone who likes me for me, not me for how he can shoehorn me into what he wants."

"And, in the meantime, you're going to get with this cop."

"I'm sorry, but when did I become Casual Rebound Sex Girl?"

"When have you ever had anything to rebound from?" Jayne paused, presumably for me to jump in and agree with her. "The answer is never. In high school you were too busy dealing with the daily emotional fall out from your mother. Then we went to college and you were Over Achiever Girl. The guys you dated were convenient and casual and gone quicker than I could be bothered to remember their names.

"Yeah, because those eight-months with Marcus sophomore year just flew by."

"*My point* is that you've never come out of anything serious which would lead to the need for rebound."

"I don't need to rebound now either. I was over Jason before I even got home that night."

"Because you woke up. But, that doesn't mean you don't need to reset your palate."

"I'm sorry, but guys aren't coffee."

"And isn't that just the biggest shame of anything we've discussed today? And not my point." I hear her keyboard clicking away in the background. "I'm looking at this, and Kasey I have to say you must be—" Jayne gasped and then let out a long *awwww*. "Look! A kitten."

"What are you doing? Are you on the Officer Max hashtag?"

"Oh, this one is great too. He's literally helping a little old woman cross the street." A long moment and then another click. "Oh, nice. Here he's in those little shorts and t-shirts cops and military train in. He's doing some charity obstacle course race. Did they hose him down for this?"

I focused all of my willpower on not getting online and looking at these pictures. After the dreams—I mean, nightmares—last night with Max and kittens, the last thing I needed was a wet t-shirt Max and kittens follow-up tonight.

"Jayne."

"I'm just saying, the boy is hot. Hot is good."

"Hot typically comes with a whole bunch of—"

"Oh! *Who is that?*"

Since I was working hard to not check out whatever site she was looking at all these pictures on, I really had no idea. But I could guess.

"Auburn hair, blond streaks, glasses? Has that whole, *I sail on the weekends, but I'm really just a JCrew kinda guy* look going on?"

"Yeah, him. And probably the best looking guy I've seen in my life."

"Oh. I haven't met Best Looking Guy #1, but the other guy is Jenna's boyfriend, Ben."

"I really need to come visit you."

"I'm so glad that where my personal tragedies couldn't win a visit from you, the fact that I'm currently surrounded by hot guys does."

"I'm shallow, but you love me anyway."

"No pressure, but..." I'd never asked before and I couldn't help but wonder how much of that was that I didn't want to put her on the spot, how much was that I was afraid she'd say no, and how much was that I knew she'd rock the boat with Jason.

Somehow I'd never connected the fact that I knew she didn't like him, and the two of them together for more than an afternoon would be a disaster, and the fact that it was him I was embarrassed by.

That's not quite the right word. Not embarrassed. I mean, he was good-looking and smart and successful. Maybe I knew deep down that I would be embarrassed by being with him.

"Maybe," I continued, "you could come visit?"

There was a pause on the other end and I knew she was thinking of a way to let me down lightly. I shouldn't have asked. I knew better. I wasn't the type of person people sacrificed for. Even my oldest friend. I knew better than to put someone on the spot like that.

Finally, in a voice softer in more ways than one, Jayne answered, "I thought you'd never ask."

"What?"

"Well, the two times I was there, Jason didn't exactly love me and I didn't want to put you on the spot where you felt you had to play referee or that you had to pick, so I figured you'd just...you know. We'd keep in touch and I'd see you whenever you came home."

I closed my eyes and set my head down on the table in front of me, shocked and embarrassed by the truth I could hear in her words.

"I wish I'd known you felt that way."

"Nah. You wouldn't have been able to handle it while you were being *mentored*." Jayne laughed on the other end of the line, breaking the tension. "But, honey, you're a graduate now and we're going to find you a professional."

Ignoring the fact that her metaphor basically had me hiring a male prostitute, I was already mentally preparing for Hurricane Jayne to land.

FIFTEEN

SOMEWHERE A PHONE was ringing.

It wasn't my cell phone, so at first I was going to ignore it, but it just kept ringing. Then it stopped and started again.

I didn't want to go all horror movie on myself, but...it was coming from inside the house.

Finally, I snuck into the kitchen—which was hard seeing as I could basically see the entire kitchen from my bed with the bedroom door open—and found a landline next to the fridge.

Should I answer it? Technically it was my phone now, but I didn't even know there was a landline. Maybe it was someone who really needed to get in touch with Ben and if I didn't answer it he'd never know his uncle three times removed who he'd never met before had died and left him a castle in Ireland.

Obviously, I needed to answer the phone.

Holding it to my ear as if it might explode, I almost whispered, "Hello?"

"Kasey?"

Someone knew my name. Maybe I had a stalker. That would pretty much round this week out well.

"Who is this?"

"It's Max."

My brain stalled out for a moment, first with, *Max who?* Then with, *Oh my gosh, Max calling me? He knows about the kittens.*

Then sanity returned.

Well, as sane as I'd been lately.

"Hey, Max. What's up?" Smooth.

"I was just calling to make sure you remembered to have the locks changed."

I stared at the phone wondering what alternate reality I'd stepped into.

"Um, what?"

"You know the locks. How Ben said he wasn't sure who had his old keys? As a woman alone, you want to make sure you know where all the keys are."

"Right. It's on the list." And the list was the size of an old New York City phone book.

"How far down the list exactly is it?" He sounded suspicious. Like he didn't believe there was a list or if there was this wasn't actually on it.

I bit my tongue and stopped the *Why is that your business* question from slipping out.

"Somewhere. It's on there somewhere. But, then again so is buying food so I don't starve to death, remembering to put clothes on when I leave the house so I'm not arrested, and to give up drying my hair in the bathtub." I sucked in a breath, trying to keep my voice even. "You know all that life stuff that keeps you from being dead."

I thought Max would have a witty retort right away, but the phone stayed silent for a moment. I almost said, "Max?" but part of me was hoping he'd just given up, set the phone down, and walked away.

"I'm just trying to help." He didn't sound apologetic. He didn't sound annoyed. He sounded like this was just a statement of fact.

I had a sad feeling that he'd call anyone he met one day previously to make sure she changed her locks.

"Thanks Max. But, I got this." I wish I could say something like, I've been taking care of myself for years. But before the words came out of my mouth I knew they weren't true. Even when I was taking care of my mom and her issues, she was at least enough of a parent to make sure I was fed and clothed and going to school. Her stuff was emotional balance. She wasn't a crappy parent. Then four years of undergrad living in the dorms because it was easier and cheaper. Then off to grad school where I soon fell into the habit of following Jason's lead.

Making a list would probably be a good idea. I scrambled around looking for a notebook. I had a feeling trying to keep it on my phone would crash the system.

"Okay." He drew the word out and I knew there was more coming. "Have you sent a change of address form to the post office?"

"Max. *Really*. I got this." All thoughts of fluffy kittens harbored in the safety of Max's arms flew out of my head. Also, I added *update address* to the list.

This was for the best. Between the dream and Jenna's matchmaking and Jayne's encouragement to rebound, I hadn't realized I'd been weakening. But, just when I started to think Max wasn't such a bad idea, he called a phone I didn't even know I had to remind me what a controlling guy was like.

"You know what though?" I asked. "Thank you for calling. It was really nice and a good reminder."

"Reminder?"

"I'll see you around. Have a good one."

Before he could ask any more questions or give me any more safety initiatives about how to live my own life, I hung up.

Guy, gone.

And that's how he was going to stay.

SIXTEEN

THE NEXT DAY, after breaking my back unpacking—and yes, getting the locks changed and emailing the post office—I packed up my laptop and headed over to The Brew to get some work done.

Ah, free wifi. The mating call of every self-employed startup on the planet.

"Back again, Mocha?" Abby looked at me in what I assumed was supposed to be a welcoming expression. "Still wearing those yoga pants everywhere, huh?"

I bit my tongue. It was going to be swollen by the end of the week if I kept having to deal with all these opinionated life-runners. I may not be ready to tell them to leave me alone, but at least I wasn't letting them shove me around any more.

"Abby. Lovely to see you. You're looking fresh as a daisy. Yes, a mocha would be great. I'll just put my work over by the comfy chairs and be back when you're done with my drink." I gave her my super big smile. "Then we can just skip whatever today's lecture would have been."

Flashing her a syrupy smile, she rolled her eyes before I pivoted to head toward what I had decided was My Chair. Pulling the coffee table closer, I laid out my to do list and the list of potential people to contact about jobs. I needed to update LinkedIn, but I sure as anything wasn't going near Facebook knowing Jason was bad mouthing me there. Why bother?

The whirl of the coffeemaker brought a smile to my face and I considered where I was going to find more clients just so I could afford to work here.

I paid for my drink, ignoring Abby as much as possible and settled into work.

Domain name, check.

Domain email contact form, check.

Price sheet, check.

Website set up sketched out, check.

LinkedIn profile created, check.

See, this wasn't so hard.

I also had several people I needed to contact right away. It wasn't exactly stealing clients, but it was staying in touch. Not that it mattered. I knew the people who would have hired my old company, Brockman, weren't the same ones who would take a chance on a one woman start up.

Basically, a message saying that I was free and if they knew someone who was looking to hire a boutique shop to do specialized work, I would love to speak with them.

If I couldn't sell myself, I wasn't much of a marketing person, was I?

I was wrapping up my final draft of the press release when a slight body dropped into the chair across from me.

"I was hoping you'd be here." Jenna waved to John and started building a small office around her with a laptop and note cards and post-its and note cards and...basically everything but her desk.

"Tree still in your office?" Which, now that I was getting to know her, that made so much more sense and wasn't surprising in the least bit.

"Nope. The tree is gone, now I just need a roof and wall." She pulled her wallet out and headed toward the counter to order. When she got back, she propped her feet on the edge of the battered table and looked me over. "How goes the new company?"

"Not bad. My website went live and I'm about to email all my contacts to let them know I'm a free agent."

"Nice. Any bites already?" Jenna looked so hopeful, I almost hated to try to explain to her that I was basically one failure away from eating Ramen.

"Not yet, but I haven't sent out most of the mailing. I've only changed my LinkedIn, and it's early. I'll send the press release after lunch when people are back but their morning stuff is off their plate."

"Ooohhh. A plan. I love it!"

Abby walked Jenna's drink down and plopped it down in front of her. "You know, this isn't a wait service situation. Feel free to not make me walk over here."

"Abby, the six feet isn't bad for you. And, you could have just shouted at me if you didn't want to walk it over."

Abby rolled her eyes again, set the drink down and wandered off as if Jenna hadn't just reprimanded her. I was beginning to think that was Abby's version of a smile.

"So," Jenna dove right in as I set up, "have you looked at my website yet? Do you know what you'd do?"

I'd actually spent the night before looking at it and reading her books' reviews on Amazon to get a feel for not only how she saw her books, but how her readers saw them.

"Yup. And I have a few questions I'd like you to answer before I move forward."

I handed her my client questionnaire that was basically a tuned up version of the one I'd created for Brockman. "This will help me know what your vision is if you have one, how open you are to something new, what your limitations are, and where you may not know you need help. Skip the budget questions."

"Why am I skipping the budget question?"

"You're obviously on a separate payment plan. I'm willing to do a complete overhaul for you for a discounted amount so you can be one of my portfolio sites." I named a price I thought was probably fair for everything she'd done for me and would still make my time worth it with the portfolio option.

"Kasey, that's not even half of what I paid to have the site created in the first place."

I tried to keep my disgust off my face since her site wasn't worth twice what I was charging her to begin with.

"We'll build into this a payment structure for updates and maintenance. Not to worry, you'll be paying me for years to come to manage this for you if you don't get an assistant."

That was my plan. To construct a company that was more than just a design studio. I was building a one-stop partnership where the care and management of your marketing assets were key, so a small business didn't need to grow their marketing department. Not to mention, I'd have a constant flow of business.

"That sounds good." Jenna paged through my printouts. "I mean, every time I had a new book come out it was like pulling teeth to get the site updated. I'd like to find someone who I could depend on to make sure things are seamless."

"That's me. Seamless."

"Perfect. And, you can tell me all about it tonight at game night."

Um..."Game night?"

"Right. I'm having people over to chill out and relax after the crazy week. We're going to play Taboo. Three teams of two."

I was starting to get suspicious of where this was going. "People?"

"You know, me and Ben, and then you, Hailey, Dane, and Max."

I wasn't fooled by her casual chatter or the order she'd put the names in.

"Really?"

"Yup. Just a couple friends hanging around, eating pizza, playing some games." She smiled that smile I'd become completely suspicious of over the past week. We should use her to gather intel. Foreign operatives would never see what hit them.

"I'm not sure, Jenna. I have a lot going on. I should probably get some more work done tonight." And avoid the matchmaking. "I've got this new client. She's looking for a big overhaul of her site."

"Oh, come on." Now it was Jenna's turn to roll her eyes. "You've already gotten a ton done and you have your first client. Aren't you supposed to be working to keep your clients happy? I want you to come to game night. That will keep me happy."

"Yeah, that's not going to work on me. I've already seen the need to draw lines with you. I'm not ending up a hashtag."

"You can't blame a girl for trying." She grinned. "But, still, game night. You need to come. Don't think now that you're moved in you get to get rid of us that easily. It will be fun. And you can meet Hailey. You'll like her a lot. She writes YA too. And Dane. Even if you don't like him, you'll enjoy looking at him. Come on, Kasey. Don't go all fringe friend on me already."

The truth sat there between us, as true for me as I expected it was for her. I *liked* Jenna. I did need more girlfriends...more friends period. And, she seemed to feel the same way. There was no reason to think that New Kasey couldn't control the situation and not fall into some type of accidental dating situation with a guy just because he was hot.

It's not like Max had shown any interest in me.

"Sure. Game night. Count me in."

I started thinking about walls and how high they needed to be as I settled back in to get the rest of my list done.

I'm guessing with Jenna, six stories might not be high enough.

SEVENTEEN

J ENNA, WHAT PART OF *no* do you not understand?"
Max's voice pushed its way through the front door of
the condo, a little more forcefully than I would have
expected for a game night chit chat.

"I'm not telling you to date her. I'm just saying she's really
nice and super cute. Don't think I didn't notice you checking
her out."

"Checking her out is one thing. Taking her out is
completely different. I'm not dating someone who needs to
be managed that much. She can't walk across town without
creating A Situation."

I could even hear the capitals on the last two words.

Who the hell did Max think he was judging me on a
couple bad days? It's not like I was throwing myself at him
like all those girls on Twitter...and probably half of them
around town too.

"Right. Sure. Like I said, you don't have to date her. Just
be nice and make her feel welcome." I could picture the look

on Jenna's face while she humored Max and I doubt I liked it any more than he did.

"Listen to my words, Jenna. I—"

That was enough of that. I knocked on the door, thankful for the silence that fell from the other side followed by light footsteps rushing over.

"Kasey! I'm so glad you're here." She pulled me into a hug while clicking the door closed behind me with a solid thud.

Behind her, Max stood, hands in his pocket as he leaned against a kitchen island. "Kasey." He gave me a curt nod.

Yeah. Game night. Fun.

"Kasey!" Ben strolled out of a back room, obviously comfortable with the new living arrangement after one night. "We're so glad you could come. We haven't had even teams in..." .

The fadeout wouldn't have been that interesting if it hadn't been accompanied by a glance in Max's direction.

That was interesting.

No. No, it wasn't. I wasn't interested in anything to do with Max. No matter what Jayne said about him being hot or the weird Kitten Calendar Dream.

But then a horrific thought crossed my mind. "What about the other people?"

"Hailey got caught up writing and she's running a few minutes late. Dane shows up when he wants." Jenna started putting together a fruit tray, completely focused on not meeting my gaze. "Which will be almost on time since I threatened to post his dating history online if he didn't start being more considerate of his friends."

She was not someone to cross. Amazing how she balanced being so sweet with the tiny, little dictator who peeked out occasionally. "You guys head into the living room and make yourselves comfortable."

I smiled at Max, annoyed at how much he didn't want to date me. Not that I wanted to date him. But he didn't have to be so vocal about how uninterested he was in me. I turned toward the other end of the open set up where a set of overstuffed living room furniture made a welcoming corner.

"So..." I glanced around looking for something to say that didn't scream *I heard you talking about how repulsive you find me*. It was harder to come up with than you'd think. "Did you work today?"

"Yup."

"Anything interesting happen today?"

"Nope." He settled in the chair across from me. "So I'm assuming you didn't leave the house?"

I could feel my shoulders stiffening up. "No. I did. You may want to check the local banks."

The corner of his lips quirked up and he glanced back toward the kitchen. "I probably would have heard about a bank being robbed."

"I'm that good, obviously. You won't find out for another week or so. But, don't worry. I'll keep your name out of it when they bring me in for questioning."

Max shook his head, the smile still fighting those lips I definitely wasn't looking at. Just as he opened his mouth to reply, the front door flew open.

"Sorry I'm late, but look who I found hitting on one of your neighbors in the lobby."

I turned toward the voice and...stalled out.

The most stunningly good-looking guy I'd ever seen stood in the doorway behind an unconventionally pretty girl, a grin on his face that showed he was absolutely not feeling guilty about being late so he could flirt with some stranger.

He moved into the room, a gait made to watch, and hugged Jenna before shaking Ben's hand. I'd lost track of the girl who'd come in with him while watching him move. It was a thing of beauty.

"Great. Another one drops under the supercilious good-looks of the playboy." Max kicked one leg up to cross the ankle over his knee and leaned back in the chair studying me as if he'd have to file a report at the end of the evening.

"What?" I knew what he was talking about, but I wasn't stupid enough to admit to it.

"Dane. You're reacting just like every other girl does when she sees him. Now he's going to spot you, a new girl in the room, sashay over, and flatter you into falling at his feet."

"I'm sorry." I shook my head at Max as he started to look surprised at my apology. "I didn't realize guys sashayed. Is that a new thing or is it just a Dane specific swagger?"

"Oh, he's got tons of swagger. Everywhere we go he manages to use it to the best of his advantage."

"Jealous?"

"That he's going to come in here and see if you're stupid enough to fall for it like ninety-five percent of the female population?" Max gave a small snort as if answering wasn't even worth his time.

"Obviously you're not jealous that he might try to hit on me. I mean, why would you be interested in someone who keeps creating *situations?*"

Max's arms dropped to his side, a blush creeping up his neck.

"Listen." He leaned forward, even as he glanced away. "I didn't mean to be insulting. I just...you're not my type. It's not you."

"Don't worry about it. It's not like I'm sitting here throwing myself at you. I think you're safe."

"No. Kasey. It's..." He glanced toward the kitchen where Jenna was mixing drinks and obviously keeping everyone very busy while Max and I sat in the living room falling in love—at least, I'm pretty sure that's what she was convinced was happening. "It really isn't you. I just got out of something a while ago and she was a bit too wild for me. I'm not looking, but when I am, I'll be looking for someone a little less...complicated than you are. Not that there's anything wrong with that. It's just not what I'm looking for."

He studied me as if I were going to burst into tears at this announcement. Who was the cocky one in the room? I glanced toward Dane, awed again by his gorgeousness and wondered.

"Don't worry, Max. You're totally not my type. I get the not-personal thing. You're the last guy I'd date, so you're safe from me."

He nodded, his smile still looking forced. "Well, good."

We sat there, an awkward silence between us as I watched the foursome in the kitchen.

"Why not?"

My gaze drifted back to Max. "Excuse me?"

"Why not?"

"Why not, what?" He really could not be asking what I thought he was.

"Why am I not your type?"

"You're kidding me, right?"

"Yeah." He paused and looked toward the kitchen again. "Well, kind of. You know, I'm just curious. Nothing more. Just wondering why...you know."

"Why I'm not interested in dating you?"

"Yeah. That."

Guys are crazy. They talk about how nuts women are, but this was exactly the type of thing that proved they were far less sane than we are.

"I don't need any more alpha male crap in my life. I'm starting over. This is my chance to be my own woman and not stand in some guy's shadow who's going to tell me what the best way to live my life is and shoe horn me into his. I want someone interested in the same stuff and looking for the same lifestyle. I don't need a guy who is, you know..."

Now he wasn't looking so embarrassed. He was looking a little annoyed.

"No. I don't know. What?"

"Come on, Max. Not only would you expect to tell me what to do all the time, but you're a cop. How much could we really have in common? You're all walking the street fighting crime and I'm more interested in designing stuff and making time for foreign films."

"Foreign films?" He was looking at me as if I'd just said I was going to fly to the moon. "What's the last foreign film you saw?"

Was this a test?

Crap, what was the last foreign film I'd seen? I can't even remember the last movie I'd seen. Did British films count? Actually, I'd snuck out to see that X-Men film Jason refused to see based on it being *pop culture trash that was skewing the American view of politically acceptable behavior.*

"Do you even really like foreign films?" He asked, all but calling me a liar.

That was a good question? Did I? And, why did he sound like Jayne suddenly?

"Maybe. But, if I do then I want a guy who is going to see them with me."

"Any guy you date should do stuff you enjoy with you. Even if it's a suck-it-up situation. Every once in while he'd go to the cinema with you."

"Fine. If I wanted to see foreign films, you'd suck it up and go with me. Got it."

"I like foreign films. I've been looking forward to that new French film about the Riviera in the 40s and the writer's movement that went on there."

"Great. We could go see that." As soon as I said the words, I was annoyed with myself. "If we were dating. Which we're not. Because you think I'm annoying and complicated and I'm resetting my life on my own."

"Right." He re-crossed his arms and leaned back.

"So, we'll just, you know, not date."

"Good."

"Great."

Perfect.

~~*~~

"I said, *blue* not *moo*. I don't even know how you could confuse the two." I glared at Max ready to throw the board game at his head. "Is it your hearing or your listening that's the problem?"

Across the table, Dane snorted and Hailey, a sweetly sarcastic girl I liked immediately, elbowed him.

"Maybe if I weren't wondering what type of chaos you were going to rain down any second I would be able to focus on the game more."

A low, *oooohhhh* whispered from the silent pair at the end of the coffee table.

"And yet, the only thing that's happened is the huge loss we seem to be having because of your inability to listen."

"I'm listening." Max shot back. "I'm also hyper aware of any other disasters that could strike at any moment when you're present."

"Oh, yeah?" Snappy come back there, Kasey.

"Yeah. I—"

"That is enough." Jenna stood up and threw the decorative pillow she'd been holding down. "If you two are going to ruin game night, you can both go home."

Oh, no. I was ruining game night. I glanced around the group knowing I'd just worn out my welcome. I made it through almost half a week with new friends and look what I did.

I was the wrecker of all things good.

"I'm so sorry." I tried not to literally wring my hands, but they were hanging there at the end of my arms doing nothing. "I don't know what came over me."

"I do." Hailey said and nodded her head toward Max.

Dane snorted again. "Yeah, not yet."

My gaze shot toward Max and watched as his neck slowly stained red as he glared Dane down.

"You know what?" I set down my drink and stood. "I'm really sorry. I'm just...tired. I'm going to head out. Thanks so much for having me."

"No." Jenna picked up her pillow again and threw it at Max, taking him by surprise and knocking him upside the head. "You don't have to go."

"It's okay. You guys finish the game. I'm just going to go get some rest. Thanks."

I rushed toward the door, knowing it was rude even as I did it. I felt like crying for the first time since everything that had happened. I had no idea what had gotten into me. Max Darby just rubbed me the wrong way and I was letting him get to me. I don't know why. You'd think after years of not noticing how horrible Jason was, Max's little nudges wouldn't bother me.

I pushed through the foyer's door and had to take a moment to figure out which way was home. With my luck, I'd just start walking and end up at my old place. I'd made it halfway down the block, before I heard the footsteps rushing after me.

"Tuesday!"

Yeah. Like I was going to answer to that.

"Kasey!"

Okay, I should answer to that, but I just wanted to get home. I was blowing Step One of my Begin Again plan. Unless it had magically become, *New Friends...tick them off.*

Then I was all, *Check!* on that one.

"Kasey, wait." Max caught up with me and slowed to match my steps.

I looked up at him, not wanting to apologize to the guy who nagged me into humiliation. I knew it was on purpose.

Every time I said something he had a comeback. Everything I did he insisted on the opposite. It was as if he'd spent the night trying to drive me out. Well, out I was. I'd apologized for my part of it, but that's as far as I was going.

I just shook my head and continued down the street, enjoying the crisp evening air.

We walked on, Max at my side, the street quieter than the early evening bustle of when I'd arrived.

"You don't have to walk me all the way home."

"Yes, I do."

"Actually, I'd rather you didn't."

He stopped. Just stopped. I couldn't tell whether it was because I'd offended him—again—or if he was just taking me at my word.

I decided to believe it was the latter. I walked the blocks, listening to the sounds of the city during the evening. The birds that seemed to come out of nowhere as I got closer to the tree-lined neighborhood. The cars got nicer…and quieter. I hadn't thought there were peaceful places right in town. But The Village gave that idea a run for its money.

And that's why I heard the quiet, steady steps half a block behind me, walking along, measured with mine. There was no tingly spine or nervous twitches. I knew, just knew it was Max back there making sure no one else was following me home.

When I got to my building, I climbed the elegant arched staircase and turned back to see him standing in the tree-shadowed spot under a streetlight waiting for me to go in. I raised my hand, annoyed through my thankfulness, and watched as he stood there stubbornly waiting for me to head inside.

Part of me wanted to stay there, waiting him out and see what he'd do. But, goodness knew Max was obstinate. He'd probably wait until I got all the way up to Ben's apartment and he saw the lights go on before heading home.

After climbing the steps to my new front door, I was tempted to slip inside and try to make my way among the boxes to the window and watch for his reaction to the long darkness. But, with my luck, I'd get close to the window before tripping over something and taking a header out my new third story home.

Then Max would probably have to do something and there'd be paperwork. That's all I needed to be.

More paperwork.

EIGHTEEN

W HEN MY ALARM clock went off the next morning, I asked myself why I was still bothering to set it. If my life was going down the toilet, I should at least get to sleep in. I rolled over, slamming my hand down on the snooze button and settled back in under my blanket.

I lay there, contemplating the night before and wondering if I should go back to The Brew to work. As soon as the thought crossed my mind, I was reenergized. I had work to do. I had a new business I was passionate about. Yes, I may have isolated my new friend, but life wasn't over. I was no worse off than five days ago. Although, that whole *don't know whatcha got until it's gone* thing was feeling true.

I got up and checked my email. Three people I'd sent my press release to had already responded letting me know they were disappointed I no longer worked at Brockman and promising to pass my name on to any smaller businesses looking to hire a capable boutique.

Well, that was a win. I figured if they didn't mean it, they'd just hit the delete button.

Checking out my website stats, I had twenty-two hits from the mailing. Not bad for a weekend.

Pulling myself out of my pity party, I headed toward the shower, my mind already racing with how I'd take over the marketing world. Or at least a tiny corner of it.

At the sidewalk, my feet automatically turned and headed toward The Brew. It was what it was. And also, since it was a Sunday maybe Jenna would be taking the day off. I wouldn't have to run into her and see if she was as annoyed as I thought she might be because of me ruining game night.

I pushed through the front door, sucking in the sweet smell of blended drinks and baked chocolate treats and stalled out.

Not only was Jenna there, but all of them were sitting around the little beat-up coffee table drinking frothy beverages and eating scrumptious desserty breakfast things.

Crud.

Jenna caught my eye, but before she could say anything I gave a little wave and headed to the other side of the room. I pulled out my laptop and set it up making it obvious I was there to work. Work was why I was there. Yup. There was work to be done.

Not that work was a lie, but I wanted it super clear that I had things to do.

I really didn't need a pity invite over to their cool kids' table.

Before I could finish setting up, Jenna slid into the seat across from me.

"Hey."

It was that smile. She used it like a weapon. Oh, she looked sweet. She looked like one of the nicest people on the planet. But then she gave you that smile and made it so you couldn't say no to anything she suggested.

I was going to say no. I was going to be strong and say no.

"Hi." I used my own smile like a weapon.

Or, at least I thought I did, but when Jenna looked at me like I could possibly be deranged, I wished I had a mirror.

"So, you're working today?" She glanced at the table I'd taken over with my mock ups, potential customer list, and to-do sheets.

"Yup. You know, trying to get everything up and running seems to be two full-time jobs. I think I'm dreaming business plans." I smiled when she laughed. "I woke up in the middle of last night and had dreamed I'd written my next to-do list. Only when I got up this morning the list said, Call Santa and request more work before Christmas, make green pancakes, and walk backward everywhere once a week to tighten your butt."

She was laughing at me before I got past Santa.

"So, you made a real to-do list and then came here?"

"That is the real to-do list."

Jenna shook her head at me and leaned over the table. "Are you going to come have breakfast?"

I glanced over her shoulder to where the others sat chatting and caught Max as he glanced away, that inscrutable look on his face again.

"I thought maybe...no." I shuffled my pages around trying to stall. Trying not to fall prey to the Jenna Smile. "I mean," How do you say this? "Aren't you mad at me?"

"Mad at you?" She sat up, obviously surprised. "Why would I be mad at you?"

"I ruined your game night."

This time, Jenna laughed so hard I thought Ben was going to come check on her.

"Ruined game night. Oh, that's rich." She wiped her eyes and gave me a softer, less threatening smile. "Last month Hailey threw a remote at Dane and gave him a black eye because he wouldn't stop looking down her shirt. The month before that Dane brought a *girlfriend* with him who didn't know the difference between right and left and kept having to stop and ask. He eventually wrote her a little note card and she still couldn't remember. The month before that the guys ended up in a brawl basically because in Apples to Apples Ben thinks the funny answer is right, Dane thinks the stupidest answer is right, and Max kept getting angry because he thinks the answer closest to the original card is right and they were just messing with him. They broke my favorite yard sale bowl. The month before that—"

"Are you making this up?"

"Even I couldn't make this up." Jenna glanced over her shoulder before turning back to me, leaning in, and lowering her voice. "My friends are kind of crazy. I'd like to blame Ben and his friends, but I'm pretty sure mine aren't any better."

"I kind of doubt you were being nice to me to up the sanity ratio."

"Oh, heck no! I just figured you'd fit right in."

My eyes fell shut and I pictured it. I pictured fitting in. I pictured game nights and breakfasts and Shakespeare in the Park and holidays and celebrations and life. But the problem was, even as each picture shifted and the players moved, there was one constant. There, next to me, giving me that look halfway between his inscrutable stare and his dimple-blessed smile was Max Darby.

He'd tick me off then make sure I lived through another day. Talk about extremes.

I let my gaze drift over to the table again and wondered if I *could* fit in. With Jenna, yes. With the guys and Hailey, maybe. But with Max…I didn't know.

It was like he wanted to keep his distance and still be the boss of me.

"Come on." She reached down and started shuffling my papers together. "You have to eat breakfast anyway. You might as well come over and put up with us."

I glanced back over at the group wondering if they had seen my Situations like Max had, they'd be keeping their guard up with me too.

Jenna stopped, and set my stuff down. "I mean, you don't have to. If we're a little much for you, I totally get it." She let out a little awkward laugh, her eyes dropping to the side. "We're a little much for me sometimes too."

It took me a minute to realize it *wasn't me*.

For years whenever something went wrong, Jason would sweetly take the time to explain why something hadn't been the best idea or how maybe I might not want to word things a certain way. He'd do it about work too. He'd hear a story about work and assume I'd handled it in the worst possible way. He'd give me advice—lectures—about why I needed to be more patient and more influencing.

I'd once brought my yearly review home to show him how my boss had called me one of the most patient managers he'd ever had. How I was excellent at reading people and situations.

It did no good.

When we fought, Jason always let me know he forgave me. Even when he admitted he might have *read me wrong*...apparently the closest thing to *it was my fault* he could get.

I stood there, in the warmth of the coffee shop, realizing again that since I'd been a grad student basically off the bus from Ohio, Jason had been molding me into what he wanted and I'd lost more than my identity. I'd lost my ability to see my value and the weight of my own actions.

"Kasey?"

I snapped back to today, reminding myself I wasn't there any more. Reminding myself that if I didn't want to be that girl now, I was the only one who could control that.

I was the boss of me. I took ownership of my actions. I was not valued by who was standing next to me.

I glanced over to the group again, all of them relaxed back into their overstuffed chairs with their sweet breakfast drinks and knew I wanted to be part of that. Max shifted, his gaze colliding against mine and his brows drawing down just a bit in the middle.

"Sure. Of course, I'd love to join you guys." I packed up my stuff and followed her over, feeling a little embarrassed by the fact that they'd caught me trying to not hang out with them now that I knew I was welcome.

"Hey, trying to escape us, huh?" Dane stood and took my bag, placing it on the floor next to the empty chair. "What can I grab you?"

"Oh, no. Don't worry. I can get it." The last thing I needed was to feel obligated to him for buying me a drink…which I know how 1987 that sounded.

"It's no problem. You were a great sport last night. The least you can do now is let a guy buy you a drink."

He said it so smoothly I was betting that's how he usually handled his pickups at a bar too. And who was I to ignore the charm that is Dane?

"Well, since you put it that way." I gave him my order and he swaggered—I mean, sashayed—off to hook me up. I'm not going to lie, I watched him go. The guy knew he was absurdly good-looking and used it to his advantage. We ladies might as well get the advantage of watching him so it evened out a little.

Next to me, someone cleared his throat. When I say *someone* I mean, Max.

"Yes?"

"Just making sure your neck wasn't stuck."

"Nope. Just making sure he gets the drink order right." I gave him a sticky sweet smile which he managed to scowl at.

"Sure. Right." He brought his mug to his lips and shifted his focus back to the café as a whole.

The group chatted about upcoming events and work and dates. I slowly began to pick up on their inside jokes and felt a few I could even laugh at after the night before.

"So, Kasey, how's the new company going?" Hailey leaned forward to chat with me around Dane. Instead of leaning back to give her space, he started playing with her hair where it fell over his leg.

I wondered if they were an item. Some type of weird off-and-on thing maybe. That would so never be me. I wouldn't be some guy's hookup no matter how hot he was. My gaze darted back up to Dane again as I rethought that. Maybe…

No.

Nope.

Not gonna happen.

I mean, besides the fact that he was *Dane.*

"Not bad." I refocused. Ignore the pretty boy. Ignore him. I glanced the other way. Ignore the scowling boy too. "Besides Jenna's rebranding, I have two other small gigs. Unfortunately, one is a time suck for how big it actually is."

"What is it?"

"I'm creating branded packages for weddings for a planner. She wants to have a couple of pre-created packages that are just for her clients. So, save the dates, invites, event websites, etcetera. Each can be slightly customized by things like color, but mostly they'd all be the same. She likes the idea that even though they're all the same, no one else has them."

"That's actually pretty cool."

"And extremely exciting, right?" I tried not to snort. I wasn't exactly in happy wedding mode, so it had been an odd request. But I'd worked with Mae years ago when she did event planning for Brockman and she said she'd always liked the work I'd done. She hadn't even been on my contact list, but had heard about my new business through the grapevine and wanted to grab me while I was still *available, desperate, and affordable.*

Here's hoping that didn't last long.

"Still, it sounds like she's letting you be creative." Hailey seemed to be the one of the group who was most creative-focused.

Jenna's writing came from the fact that in her head her written world was real. It was almost *un*creative the way she worked. She was more, as she described it, a transcriptionist of the crazy things her characters were doing.

Hailey, from listening to her last night, liked the process. She also seemed to be more down to earth than Jenna. She'd asked me for ways to do PR without leaving her house. The idea of having her picture taken with person after person or speaking in public or—as she put it—speaking to an empty room, were not on her favorites list. She just wanted to write her stories.

After she and Dane had wandered into the living room last night while Jenna and Ben finished up in the kitchen, Hailey had immediately chatted me up, asking me what I do and if I liked it. She even invited me to the gym saying she'd found a trainer who worked her just hard enough before sending her off to do yoga.

Gym. Work. Yoga.

Not three words in my standard vocabulary, but she promised to make them go easy on me and that she had a guest pass for a free week, so I knew that I was sucked in.

She was a hard woman to say no to.

As breakfast broke up, I started unpacking my work, noticing I was the only person stupid enough to be working on a gorgeous Sunday. I guess if I had a Ben or a Dane I wouldn't be working today either.

Everyone stood, hovering around and making plans for the next week when Max turned to look down at me, that crease between his eyes growing as he stood there.

"What?" I glanced down at my shirt, ninety percent sure he was staring at the mess I'd probably dropped all over me, eating that incredibly good, but ridiculously crumbly coffee cake muffin Dane had gotten me.

"That movie is playing tonight."

I rushed through all the conversations this morning. The group was famous for talking over one another, jumping between three different conversations, and basically being able to read each other's minds with a glance. I didn't remember a movie being talked about though.

"What movie?"

"The French film."

French film? French film? We'd talked about a French film?

"You know. The one about the Riviera we talked about last night?"

Oh. That film. The moment when I'd been stupid by trying to pretend I was more interesting than I was.

"Really?" Where exactly was he going with this?

He stood over me, watching everyone else leave, lifted his hand to Dane as he paused at the door and then turned back to me.

"So, I'm going to see it and thought maybe you'd like to come too." He stood watching me stare blankly at him, the crease between his eyes getting deeper. "You know, just to hang out and see if you like it. I know you're adjusting to all this new stuff. Thought you might want to take a break."

Oh. A pity hang out.

And yet, this was exactly the type of thing I wanted to try. I'd lived in this city for years and hadn't done most of the things that attracted me to it in the first place. I'd come here to try new things, experience all a city had to offer. But first I'd sunk myself into school, then work, then Jason's world.

I was sick of thinking about Jason and all the time I'd wasted.

So, yes. I did want to try a new French film.

Even if it meant trying to hang out with Max.

"Sure. What time is it?"

"I'll come get you around six-thirty."

Notice that was not an answer to my question or a suggestion.

"Actually, I can just meet you there."

"We live a block apart." More eyebrow creasing. "There's no reason for us to meet there."

"We do?" Okay, not the point. "But I have things to do, places to be, people to convince to buy my services. I won't be sitting around waiting for *le film*." Or however you'd say that in French. "So, it would be easier for me to meet you there."

Max stood, his arms crossed against his chest before he finally nodded. "Okay. I'll meet you there."

He shook his head and headed toward the door.

Um, bye?

~~*~~

"You're going out on a date with Max!"

You know, after a week you'd think I'd be used to Jenna and her anti-segue conversations. Just start in the middle at high-excitement and go.

"No. Not a date. We're just catching a movie."

"Together."

"Yes."

"At night."

"I'm sorry, did dates get limited to evening hours? No one notified me."

"Just you and Max."

"Did you want to come?" That actually sounded like a great idea. She could translate his different glares for me.

"On your date? Pfft. No thank you."

"It's not a date."

"Sure."

Wait. Wait just a second.

"How did you know we were going to the movies if you're not coming?"

"Ben called Max to see if he wanted to go for a run and he said he was going to some film I can't pronounce."

I bit my tongue. I didn't want to add to Jenna's excitement, but I definitely wanted to know if Max had invited Ben and Jenna and they just passed on coming. Maybe he'd invited everyone but I was the only person stupid enough to claim I loved foreign films without having actually seen one.

In retrospect, that was kind of snotty. I was just trying to get him to leave me alone and to point out how different we were, but with so little Max Knowledge, I'd grabbed at straws. Apparently the wrong ones.

"Okay. You don't have to come, but I'm looking forward to it."

"Because of Max." She sounded so darn smug part of me was happy to correct her.

"No. Because I'm looking forward to the movie. It's going to be really good."

I hoped.

"Yeah. Sure." In the background I heard something. "Oops. No worries. It was just a glass."

A muffled sound came over the phone before Jenna shouted. "I *am* wearing shoes. Just like we agreed. Shoes in the kitchen."

"Ben makes you wear shoes in the kitchen?"

That was absurd and controlling and completely not like the man I'd thought Ben was. Maybe the entire world of men were bossy and I definitely was glad to know that right away.

"Oh, no. Of course not. I just agreed that I would wear shoes in the kitchen because he kept rushing in and picking me up and cutting his feet when I break things. This way he doesn't have to worry."

Okay, when put like that it was disgustingly cute.

"Anyway," Jenna continued as she picked up broken glass with me listening to the occasional *ouch*. "You and Max."

"Jenna, really. There's no me and Max. First, because I just got out of what I hadn't even realized was a horrible relationship. Two, because this is Kasey-time. I'm going to do my own thing, build my company, and enjoy the city. And lastly, because I'm sure Max and I would make a horrible couple. We have nothing in common and he's exactly the type of guy I'm not looking for."

"I know, right? Who in their right mind would want a hot, kind, smart, funny, law-enforcing hunk?"

"Does anyone still say hunk?"

"You know what I mean, Kasey Lane. Max is great. You'd be really lucky to date him."

Oh crud. Now I'd insulted one of her best friends.

"You know what I mean, Jenna. Not every great guy is the right guy for you."

There was a deep sigh on the other side of the phone and I waited for the verdict.

"Ben told me to stay out of it, but I just would love to see you happy."

How could you not love that?

"I *am* happy. I hadn't realized how unhappy I was, but this is the happiest I've been since college. I'm excited about my new business. I *love* my new apartment. I'm really happy about the new friends I've been making. I'm just...I'm just not looking right now. I need to stay focused and a guy would take away from that."

"Okay. I guess I can see that." She sighed again. "But, call me after your *movie*. If it isn't too late that is."

The girl was hopeless.

NINETEEN

I STARED INTO MY recently filled closet, wondering what one wore to a foreign film at a small, independent movie theater. It sounded so hipster. I definitely lacked hipster clothing. And, I hadn't been shopping for normal clothes because my check from the consignment store hadn't come in yet.

I'd made a deal with myself that I wouldn't buy anything new until my old clothes paid for it. I'd been excited when the girl had *oohhh*'d over my suits. One thing Jason had drilled home to me that I actually agreed with was to save your money and buy good clothing for the office. Marketing was such a judgmental group. If you didn't look the part, then they believed you couldn't make other people look their part.

On the upside, I wouldn't miss having my nails done every week. I'd always thought that was a waste of money and I only liked color on my toes. Of course, I wasn't giving up my highlights.

None of this helped me pick out an outfit for the movie though.

Not that this was a date. It wasn't. But I wanted to look nice and dress right for the occasion. This wasn't for Max. I didn't want to be that girl who people looked at and thought, "What's he doing with her?"

Not that he'd be *with* me. But other people didn't know that. They'd think we were together. Like on a date. Or maybe a couple already. No, there's no way we'd give off couple vibes. So, basically I just needed to wear something that let me blend in with where I was going, what I was doing, and who I'd be with. That meant—

That meant I was *way* over thinking this.

I pulled out my favorite pair of jeans, a Guess t-shirt, and a pair of wedges it was just warm enough to wear. I grabbed a light jacket and my purse, checked the directions so I didn't look like a tourist in my own neighborhood, and headed out.

This was going to be great. It felt very sophisticated. I wondered if they served popcorn. What did sophisticated people eat at the movies? I mean, films. Whatever. Should I have brought a snack? Maybe I could still grab some peanut M&Ms to sneak in. Should I grab Max something too? No. No, Max would have to bring his own snacks. Plus, if he didn't pull out snacks then I'd know this wasn't a snack type place.

Which, really? Everywhere should be a snack place.

About a block down the street, I saw a guy sitting on his stoop, reading his phone. Of course it was Max. Shocker.

I pulled to a stop in front of him annoyed he'd obviously been waiting on me even though I'd told him I'd meet him there. This is exactly what I'd been trying to explain to Jenna.

He was too much like Jason. Everything had to be his way. He was orchestrating things how he wanted them without necessarily going against what I'd said.

I stood there, watching him, his head still bent over his phone.

He finally glanced up, no crease between his eyes this time. But, getting what you want is far more relaxing than not getting what you want.

"I'm not waiting on you. I'm texting my brother. I'll meet you there."

And then he went back to his phone.

Seriously.

Was this reverse psychology?

"Okay. I was thinking of stopping at CVS. See you there."

"'kay." Type. Type. Type.

I nodded which of course he didn't see and headed down the street.

"Kasey." His deep voice stopped me in my tracks even though, when I turned back, he was still looking at his phone. "Other way."

I glanced down the street. Yup. I'd headed back toward my place.

Trying not to huff, I pivoted and strode past him.

I got about the same distance beyond him the right way, when I heard my name again.

"Could you grab me some Junior Mints while you're at CVS?"

I gave him the sweetest smile I had, knowing at this point he had to be screwing with me.

"Sure. Anything else?"

"Nope." He went back to his phone. "Thanks."

I fumed the entire way to CVS while trying not to fume at all. What did I care if he wasn't waiting for me? It was a really nice night out. Who wouldn't want to sit outside to text a friend? It was obviously someone he was happy to chat with; the phone was dinging every time he stopped. It probably wasn't even his brother. It was probably a girl. Some really cute girl who didn't mind that he scowled at her all the time.

Or, maybe he didn't scowl at her. Maybe he only scowled at me. Not exactly the way I wanted to be special.

Not that it mattered. It was good that he was texting some girl. Then Jenna could stop worrying about him finding a nice girl or trying to set us up. Which would be great because then I wouldn't be distracted by her attempts and could focus on my career.

Exactly.

I got to CVS and grabbed my M&Ms and glared at his Junior Mints before breaking and grabbing them too.

The theater was on the same block. I headed toward it wondering if Max was still texting his super hot girlfriend and if I should head in to get us a seat. I stood in front of the building checking out the movies playing. Besides the French film, there was some Sundance winner, a blockbuster action movie, and a midnight sing-along for The Sound of Music.

Well, that narrowed down what I'd be doing one night. Midnight showing or not, it wasn't something I'd miss. I was a sucker for that movie. Every year when it was on growing up, I'd watch it with my mom. She used to try to explain to me how hot Christopher Plummer was, but I was too busy reenacting Sixteen Going on Seventeen.

"Ready?" a deep voice asked from behind me.

I guess this was close enough to count as meeting there.

"Yup."

We headed down the building to the box office, side by side.

"So, this should be good." Max tossed a grin my way. He really was excited to see the film. "I've been looking forward to this since the actor talked about doing it during his down time. Did you know he spoke fluent French? His father apparently is some French diplomat who had an affair with his super-model mother during a national summit thing."

Wow.

"Nope. Didn't know that." I'm not even sure how I would know that.

"How confident are you feeling in your French?" He asked as he pulled the door open for me. "Mine is pretty good, but the Parisian speakers lose me. If you get a little lost, just let me know. Je serai votre guide français."

I froze, trying not to panic.

"The movie is in French?"

"Yeah. Of course. It's a French film."

Crud.

Crud, crud, crud.

"Right." I glanced around as if help would come out of nowhere. "French."

Max stood there a long moment, watching my panic and probably thinking I was an idiot.

"Kasey, I'm kidding."

"It's not in French?"

"Oh, it's in French all right. It is a *French film*. But there are subtitles. You don't need to know any French to enjoy it."

"Right. Right. I knew that."

"Uh-huh."

"I did, but, you know…I thought you were going to some special non-subtitled showing with your fancy French talking self."

"Nope. Just normal subtitled showing."

"Good. Because I totally love subtitles." Kasey, shut up. Stop saying things that weren't true or that you don't know are true. Maybe I did love subtitles. I'd know in thirty minutes.

Dear universe, please let me love subtitles.

Max just looked at me, what may have been a slight tip up in the corners of his mouth, and shook his head. "Sure, Kasey. Subtitles."

At the ticket box, Max pulled out his card and offered it to the cashier. "Two for écrit sur la Côte d'Azur , please."

Um, no. Not a date.

"One."

Max looked at me, the crease coming back. "I can get it."

"I know. But so can I."

"You got my Junior Mints."

"Did I?"

He squinted at my handbag, his inability to see through leather obviously bothering him. Finally, he nodded as if he'd found what he was looking for.

"Yes. You did. You're not the kind of person to just blithely decide not to do something you said you would."

Darn it.

And a compliment.

Double darn it.

"Fine. I got your Junior Mints. But that doesn't mean you're paying for my movie."

"He can pay for my movie," an annoyed voice said from behind me.

I glanced back, wondering why all of forty-five seconds was bothering this guy.

"Really, lady. Let the guy buy your ticket. It's not like he's asking for sex." Annoyed guy swung toward Max. "You're not expecting sex, right?"

"I'm not even expecting her to walk home with me and we live almost across the street from one another."

"This is exactly why I said I'd meet you here. I can buy my own ticket."

"You don't even have a job." He all but threw his arms in the air. I swear they twitched like he was going to before he caught himself and anchored them at his sides.

"Yes. I do. I own my own business."

"Oh, boy." The guy behind us shook his head.

"You've owned your own business for the week since you lost your job."

"Oh, honey." Annoyed guy's wife reached out and laid a hand on my arm. "You lost your job? You should absolutely let this nice young man buy your ticket."

"I don't *need* him to buy my ticket." Why was I explaining myself to strangers now?

"Of course you don't," she said with a ridiculously sweet smile that was probably genuine.

Now I was the one fighting not to throw my hands in the air.

"Thank you, sir."

I spun back around as the cashier handed Max two tickets.

"Max!"

"You can buy next time."

As if I was going to hang out with him again with all the havoc he was wreaking.

We made our way toward the theater and he veered, changing direction toward the concession stand where there was definitely popcorn. This place wasn't as schwanky as I'd expected. Apparently foreign films were just like American films only with subtitles…and probably actual plot lines.

"Popcorn?"

I turned back to Max, giving up my study of the normal theater with fancier posters.

"I'll get it." I reached into my purse, to hand the woman my card before Max could out maneuver me again.

He was obviously smarter than I was giving him credit for, because he put his wallet back without a word.

"What size do you want to get?" he asked.

"Whatever size you want." I wasn't going to own up to the fact that I didn't really want popcorn since I'd gotten my M&Ms.

"You're not one of those girls who's going to say we can't have butter, are you?"

"You can have all the butter you want."

Max's cop instincts must have kicked in because he leaned against the counter, crossing those arms again. The teen girl behind the counter's gaze dropped to where his biceps tightened under the hem of his t-shirt.

"You're not going to have any popcorn, are you?"

"I'll probably have some."

"What, like a bite?"

"Probably more than *a bite.*"

"I swear, Jeannine. We need to stop coming to this theater." The voice behind me was already too familiar.

I turned around and sure enough, there was annoyed guy and his wife...Jeannine.

"Just let the man buy your popcorn. Stop being such a controlling woman. If he wants to spoil you a bit, enjoy it now. What is wrong with this generation?"

Next to him, Jeannine rubbed her hand up and down his arm. "I know, Dale. But, not everyone treats each other as well as we do. Maybe he's the kind of guy who is going to be like, I *just took you to the movies* when she asks him to take out the trash so then she has to do it herself just because they saw a movie."

"You're not that kind of jackass, are you, son?" Annoyed Dale was now looking at Max as if he was going to light into him next.

"No, sir."

"You're not taking my trash out." We were going to make that clear right now or he'd be over tomorrow to make sure the moving boxes were on the curb.

"Seriously, girl, whatever your name is. You're taking this independent woman thing too far." Annoyed Dale crossed his arms and oddly looked like an older version of Max for a moment.

"We're not even dating. We're just seeing a movie."

"Mmm-hm."

I shook my head and turned back to the counter. "Medium popcorn with butter. Also, a diet Coke."

"No diet."

"It's not for you."

"You're not getting me a drink too?"

Oh for the love of stars.

"Fine. And a normal Coke."

"Thank you."

"See," Jeannine chimed in. "That wasn't so hard. But, honey, if you really don't have a job, maybe let him pay next time."

I tried not to grit my teeth as I answered, "I *have* a job."

"Mmm-hm."

At this point, Max was actually smiling. Why was it he only smiled when ridiculousness was taking over my world?

Max took the drinks off the counter and waited for me while I got the popcorn and napkins. I followed him into the little theater and waited for him to walk to the front row. I hated the front row and so I *knew* that's where he'd go. But instead, he turned down the first set of seats and said, "Back's ok, right?"

"Sure."

Thank goodness. We finally agreed on something and it was pretty darn important in my view of the world.

We sat there, two of the only people in the room, as we snacked on all the junk food we'd brought with us.

I scrambled for something to talk about before the silence got intensely awkward. Kind of like every interaction with Max.

"Do you come to these a lot?" Yeah. Original.

"Not a lot. No one likes to come with me and most of these movies are the type you want to talk about with people later. Dane won't sit still that long and Ben would rather hang with Jenna."

"You know, you could bring Jenna too."

"She doesn't like foreign films. She says the subtitles give her eyestrain."

I looked up at the screen wondering if that was a real thing.

"But," he continued, "after about ten minutes you don't even notice them. You just start reading along and watching the action at the same time."

I love how he was still talking to me as if I'd never seen a subtitled film before. It was basically calling me a liar. Not that I hadn't lied, but still. He didn't know that.

The lights dropped and the screen filled with the first trailer. I handed Max the rest of the popcorn and eased back in my chair ready to—hopefully—enjoy the next ninety minutes.

On the upside, in a dark theater Max couldn't mock or scowl at me, so it had to be better than the walk here.

~~*~~

Before the lights came back up, I shoved the tear-drenched tissues back into my bag, hoping Max didn't notice.

That was by far one of the most moving things I'd ever seen. I couldn't believe I was missing out on all these potential amazing stories because I'd never seen a foreign film before.

Mom had held on to her bitterness and used it as an excuse to not try new things. The new things were behind her because of giving up on them to marry my dad. It was easier to not move forward.

Then, Jason had always said if he wanted to read, he'd get a book.

So, yeah.

We stood, Max picking up our trash and stuffing it in his empty popcorn bag. I should have known he wouldn't leave it sitting there. Jason always had and made fun of me for cleaning up after us. I don't care if someone is paid to do it. My trash is my trash.

We made our way out of the theater behind the small group of people who thankfully did not include Annoyed Dale and his wife, Jeannine.

"So, are we walking home together, or should I give you a head start and pretend I don't know you."

"Don't be silly."

Max just quirked an eyebrow at me and held the door open. "So, were those tears of empathy from how Simone ended her days or of joy that it was finally over?"

So, not so sneaky with the tissues. Bummer.

"The way she handled situation after situation that was thrown at her. And with such grace."

"And, the subtitles didn't bother you?" Again with the eyebrow.

"Fine. That was my first movie with subtitles. Are you happy?"

Max shrugged and then stuck an arm in front of me when we reached a crosswalk as if I were a three-year-old who might stumble out into traffic without him.

I restrained myself from pushing his arm out of the way. Or him into traffic.

"Not happy. Just…" Max looked both ways and stepped out into the street, his gaze purposefully ahead, shoulders straight back. "Just because I'm a cop doesn't mean I'm an uneducated bumpkin."

Oh.

Well.

Um.

So...

Crud.

I took a breath trying to figure out how to answer this. It wasn't that I thought that exactly, but the conversation had definitely been me trying to show him how different we are. Yes, I was a marketing manager with a master's degree from an excellent school who went to upscale wine bars. My peers dated doctors and lawyers.

I didn't know how to explain that he would very much fit in with my life as I grew up, but that I was here to become a successful city girl.

"You're a snob," he said, his gaze still straight ahead.

Well, I guess not answering didn't help either.

"I'm not a snob. I'm really not. My dad was a senior manager at the plant one town over. My mom stayed home. It's just...I saw that life. I'm looking for office hours and educated conversation and—"

"So you're saying a cop can't possibly have educated conversation?"

"No, that's not what I'm saying. But, you have to admit that people's jobs typically fall in line with their interests. I'm not into, um, cop stuff."

"Cop stuff?"

"Um, guns?"

"Guns." His voice flattened and I couldn't tell if it was because he was annoyed or trying to keep the amusement out.

"Are you not interested in guns?"

"Only if they're aimed at me."

"Oh."

"Kasey, I get it. You're not sure who you are and that makes you feel pretty unsure about who other people are. But, don't go pasting labels on people until you know them. Most people don't fit in one box."

"But, that's the thing. I don't want to be in a box."

"For a girl who doesn't want to be in a box, you sure do put yourself in one. And others." He waved me off as I started to reply. "You're working so hard at trying to be what you think a successful woman in the city is, you're bypassing finding out who you are again. But this time it's your own doing."

With that he stopped walking and stopped our non-argument argument. I hadn't realized he'd walked right by his place again and stopped at my door. He gave me a smile, a full one, and finished with, "Just make sure you know what you really want and not what you think you're supposed to want before you go chasing anything else."

Before I could reply, he'd turned on his heel and jogged across the street as the evening lights flickered on around me.

TWENTY

S O, HOW WAS your date with Max?" Hailey asked. Would one of us have to get married for this to stop?

"It wasn't a date."

I'd just gotten to the gym and my nervousness was being slightly overrun by annoyance.

"Right. So, just dinner and a movie, huh?"

"No dinner. I met him," *kind of,* "at the theater. Then we went home."

"Oooohhh. You hooked up with Max!"

"No. We went to our own homes." I glanced around, afraid the entire world was listening to this conversation. "Did Jenna put you up to this?"

"She didn't put me up to it, but she did say it would be nice to hear how it went."

"It went fine if you consider two friends going to a movie and then walking home and not talking to each other again yet fine."

"So, no post date texting?"

I stopped, trying to keep my calm and glanced at Hailey just in time to see her hide her smirk.

"You're just giving me a rough time, aren't you?"

"Am I? Am I really, Kasey?" Hailey grinned, not quit as dangerous as Jenna's, but enough that it made me wonder.

"Anyway, Max and I...Yeah. No. I couldn't think of a worse idea."

"Oh, I could."

"Really?"

I thought about the few single guys in my age box who I knew and...nope. Max was the worst idea out of all those bad ideas.

"Plus," I added. "He can't stand me."

"Yeah. A guy who can't stand you always invites you out to the movies."

"Well, it was more of a calling my bluff than an actual invite."

I hated to fess up about my stupid comment about culture or how Max called me snob...or how I was really struggling with if that were true or not. Where I came from, being a cop was one step up from working on a farm or in factory. Families were absurdly proud of sons who made it onto the force. But then, you saw those guys making the same dead-end mistakes their brothers did. Not what I wanted at all.

Hailey shook her head at me as she pushed the door to the gym open and led me inside.

"Kasey, you know where Max, Ben, and Dane met, right?"

Not really sure where this was going, I shook my head. Unless they met at a gym I was pretty sure it had nothing to do with me.

"Law school." She dropped the door as she passed through, leaving me to catch up. When I joined her at the front desk, she shook her head and turned to give me her full attention. "You did not hear this from me, and I'm not even sure I should tell you. I don't want this to become a thing, or to ever doubt you when you stop being stupid. But, how exactly did you think Max could afford to live in The Village?"

I shook my head. It wasn't something I'd thought about.

"Old money."

Well, crud. Not only had I been snotty to someone who didn't deserve it, but I'd been snotty to someone who could be snotty. You know, if snotty was okay.

And, Max, annoyingly classily, had said nothing.

"Okay, shifting you out of that panicked look, let's move on to the fun stuff! First off, I should warn you, my trainer is ridiculously fit. Don't let that freak you out. He's good at dealing with us normal people."

And with that warning, Hailey signed us in.

I was worried enough about the actual working out part of this adventure. The last thing I needed was to worry about the trainer too.

"Hailey! You're early. It's a minor miracle. If bringing a friend gets you here on time every session, I may comp her membership."

The man standing before me was pretty much perfect as far as fitness. Luckily, he wasn't gorgeous too. His hair wasn't dark enough, and he looked too angular. Also, he could really have used a dimple.

Where did that thought come from?

I pushed dimples out of my head and focused back on the fitness god standing before me.

"I'm Shawn. Hailey tells me she dragged you in here by force."

"Not quite by force." I left out the pleading that felt slightly like threats.

At least he didn't make a comment about me needing to get back in shape or lose weight.

He led us into a semi-private room and grabbed three yoga mats, motioning for us to stretch out on the floor.

"Hailey tells me you're new to working out."

He let it sit out there like I had to defend myself, politely, but still.

"I wasn't really coordinated as a kid, so instead of watching me hurt myself over and over again, my mother entered me into 4-H."

"4-H still exists?" He sounded both shocked and horrified. It was as if I'd said they had a dowry set aside for whosoever won the joust tournament for my hand in marriage.

"Um. Yeah." He continued to stare as if I could pull out digital proof or something. "You know you have 4-H here too, right?"

"*We do?*"

"For real. It's not that weird." At least I didn't think it was.

I glanced at Hailey to see if she was giving me the shock-and-awe treatment as well, but she was just leaned over flat, hands wrapped around her far foot. I looked down, way down, at my foot and thought this was going to be a very long hour.

"Okay, so ignoring the lack of sports, dance, and apparently coordination, we're going to dive right in." Shawn gave me a sunny smile I could only assume was encouragement and turned to Hailey. "Twenty minutes on the treadmill. I want you doing the speed program. Kasey, you're going to start at a walk. Add an incline and a speed jump every four minutes. I'll see you ladies in twenty."

He rolled his mat up and stuck it in the corner while I gave the treadmill a once over. It was just walking, right? How hard could walking be?

"Come on, Kasey. It's going to be fine." I had resorted to self-pep talks. "Easiest piece of equipment in the gym next to the badge scanner."

Right. Walking. I totally had this.

After a moment, I found the right combination of buttons and started moving. Piece of cake. I was born to walk. I'd been walking almost my whole life. Heck! I walked here.

I waited two minutes, and then got bored with the initial speed so I bumped it and the incline up. Seriously? I couldn't even feel the slant change even though I heard the little motor doing something to adjust my machine.

After two more minutes I was feeling pretty good and bumped both up a couple more pushes of the button. Seriously, what was so difficult about the treadmill? I walked along, just starting to get a little warm as I pumped my arm to head up the tiny hill I'd created. I was still nowhere near running like the woman two over, so maybe I could bump it up a bit more and still just be walking fast.

It was amazing what a small hill and a brisk pace could do. I found myself jogging every couple steps to get back to the front of the little belt before I might slip off the end. I was definitely kicking treadmill butt.

This was great practice if I was going to be walking more since my new place wasn't right on the train line.

I stared at the little buttons wondering if I should push them again, wondering where the line between walk and jog—a line I had *no* interest in crossing—was. And then, the new, daring Kasey decided to go for it. Real quickly I hit both buttons twice and waited to see what happened.

The treadmill rose to a no-longer-little hill and threw me over that jog line faster than Usain Bolt ran a forty meter dash.

I grabbed at the dashboard, trying to keep myself going while desperately poking at any of the buttons that might slow things down. Instead, I changed the channel on the TV I hadn't even been watching.

My legs started screaming that they couldn't take any more. I dropped one foot on the side board on my left, knowing my only chance to live through my *warm-up* was to get off this darn apparatus of torture. I lifted my opposite foot to drop it on the other runner and, of course, missed.

Then, of course, chaos ensued.

This must be what Max was alluding to.

My foot hit the treadmill and threw my body around, crashing my face into the corner of the dashboard, tossing me across to the far guardrail, before finally spitting me off the back of the darned machine where I hit the wall and slunk to a heap on the floor.

You'd think someone would have noticed. But, not so much.

The woman two treadmills down just glanced over her shoulder, then went back to her running. Hailey was faced away on the treadmill on the other side of the small room.

And the two trainers were going over something on a clipboard.

I glanced toward the entry way considering crawling through it before anyone noticed me.

"Kasey!" Shawn had rushed over before I could make my escape. "What happened?"

"Oh, you know." I grinned up at him and stretched out on the floor. "I thought I should stretch more."

"While lying in a heap on the floor?"

"It seemed like a good idea at the time."

He shook his head, obviously not believing a word I said as he glanced at the super sonic treadmill and offered me a hand up.

"Maybe that's enough cardio warm-up for you today."

He shook his head again as he stepped on the runner to reach over and shut it down, as if seeing a woman thrown from an apparatus didn't happen every day. I couldn't be the first person it had abused. There was something evily genius about it. *Look at me, so safe. All you'll have to do is walk. You know how to walk, right?* It was all to lull you into a false sense of safety.

I've got my eye on you, treadmill.

I gave the machines a wide berth as I followed him over to some huge mats like the ones we had in high school that in no way made falling easier.

Yeah, I was eyeing those too.

Hailey stood there looking at me as if she expected the roof to drop in and kill us all if I got too close.

"Are you okay?"

"Yeah. Sure. Just fine." I swung my arms about like I was loosening up to get my athletics on, but probably looked like I was trying to teach myself to fly instead. "What's next?"

Shawn glanced at Hailey who just shrugged.

She was probably thinking that new friends were expendable and, as long as they could hide the body and never told Jenna, everything would be fine.

"Okay, then let's move on to lower body." Shawn handed Hailey a set of weights that read *twenty* and then turned back and grabbed a pair that said *three* on the side. "We're going to do some squats." I want to see your butt get perpendicular with the floor. Ready?"

I glanced from my weights to Hailey's, the miniscule heft of mine making me barely notice them in my hand.

"I started with threes too." She smiled at me, a reassuring smile that was the same one she'd used when she told me I'd love working out.

I was now going to refer to this as The Lying Smile.

"Kasey, watch Hailey and then join in. We're going to do three sets of twenty."

He stood on the far side of her, pointing out how low she went, how her body stayed in a certain position, how she lifted the weights up and over her head to touch as she came out of the squat.

I figured six extra pounds shouldn't be that much over my body. I just needed to worry about not falling over. I totally had this one.

After number four, I was contemplating falling over. It seemed like the better plan.

"You're doing great." Shawn came to stand behind me, helping my arms as I came out of the squat go up and over my head. "Keep it up, that's ten. Half way done."

At twelve I was thinking about all the ice cream this meant I could eat tonight. At seventeen, I was plotting Hailey's death. At twenty I dropped the weight, barely missing my foot and thinking I was never even walking past a gym again.

"Okay, ladies, good go. Hailey, that stretch looks lazy. I want to see you really putting your arms into it." He showed me the stretch, then had me do it, adjusting my shoulder when I raised it up to my ears. "This time, Hailey does twelve and Kasey you're going to do eight."

I would not take that as a sign of failure. I'd take that as a sign of a man who could spot a woman with blunt objects at her disposal.

After two more sets, we stretched again and moved on to lunges. Then bicep curls. Then something else I blocked out from the trauma of it all. At the end, Shawn did some weird stretches on the mat with us which were oddly awkward but definitely relaxing.

"Hailey, why don't you come in tomorrow and we'll go through a whole routine?"

What the heck was that? I tried to keep my eyes a normal size, but the idea that there was even more pain and suffering in a *normal* workout seemed…sick and twisted.

And people paid for this.

I followed Hailey to the women's locker room where she washed her face and changed her t-shirt. Luckily, she'd warned me I'd want to do the same, so I was at least feeling fairly fresh as I wondered why my shirt was wet all the way through and hers was barely damp.

As we packed up, I made sure to thank Shawn and tell him good-bye since I hoped to never see him again...in the best possible way.

"Put some ice on that eye." He pointed to my eye and headed toward the next woman waiting at the entrance.

"Coffee?" Hailey asked as we headed out into the sunshine.

What I really wanted was a shower, but after all but ruining her workout, it seemed rude to turn her down since she was obviously trying to be nice.

"Sure." Because walking the four blocks to The Brew sounded great.

"I saw that."

"What?" I tried to look innocent.

"That scowl."

Now I tried not to scowl.

"The walk will help you stay loose. The last thing you want to do is sit down right away."

I was going to have to take her word on it. We headed east, walking toward The Brew with the sun overhead keeping me from cooling down too quickly.

Once we got there, she held the door open and pointed toward the couches. "I got this."

"You don't have to." I was going to offer to buy hers as a thank you for inviting me along.

"I have a feeling I have to win you back over. I'll make sure it's a large."

I wasn't going to argue with that. I collapsed on the couch and closed my eyes, hoping my muscles would start forgiving me soon.

"So," Hailey placed my drink down in front of me and settled into her chair. "What's going on with you and Max?"

"Me and Max?"

She gave me the universal girl look for *Don't play dumb with me* and waited.

"I thought we covered this."

"Yes. But now I've worn you out and gotten you carbs."

I tried scowling at her since it seemed to work for Max. She just looked at me like I was ill.

"You guys were all cozy in the corner when Dane and I got there the other night and then all that tension and fighting and then he asked you out. Seems to indicate something is going on with you guys."

"We weren't cozy. We weren't even on the same furniture. What we were was where Jenna put us. She has a matchmaking streak."

"And the tension?"

He's almost arrested me three times, didn't seem like the right answer.

"I don't know. There's just something about him that rubs me the wrong way." That was true. Sometimes I just wanted to punch him in his six pack and I couldn't even figure out why. He'd just give me that unreadable look I was convinced meant he was judging me and wondering how long it was before an actual judge was judging me.

"Really?" This seemed to intrigue her way more than I'd expected. "That's weird because Max usually puts people at ease right away."

"I find that hard to believe."

"The first time you met him he rubbed you the wrong way?"

I thought back to when he'd stepped out of that cop car and into the street lights, pulling his cap over his eyes and glancing around the ridiculousness that had become my life.

Sure I'd noticed he was hot. And yes, I was impressed with how he'd handled Jason. And of course, I'd loved that he'd seen the humor in it all.

But that was Officer Max. Just Max was a different story. Just Max seemed to see the humor in my situations far less than Officer Max did.

"Oooohhhh." Hailey leaned forward and set her mug down. "That look said a million things."

Crud.

"You're going to have to spill it at some point. That's what small groups are like. We're going to figure it out. You might as well tell me now."

I sat there knowing that if both Hailey and Jenna were at this, I'd never last more than a week. Unless I hid from them, disconnected all forms of communication, and changed my name.

"Plus," Hailey continued. "I always find things out last. You totally want me to have a leg up on Jenna on this one."

"So," I drew the word out trying to figure out how much to tell her. But, with one glance at that devious smile, I knew I was toast. "I might have met Max when he was Officer Max and Jason was Ex-Boyfriend Jackass Jason."

"Oh, this is better than I expected." She settled back into the chair and took the story as it came. At one point, she nearly snorted tea out her nose and raised a hand to stop me. "You know the *I'm a Writer Disclaimer*, right?"

"No. I got exempt from social media, but what's the Disclaimer?"

"Anything you tell me may end up in a book unless you specifically ask for it to be off the record." She glanced at her bag and I could all but see her trying to remember if she had a notebook. "I mean, that thing with the tires. That's good. That would even work with Raven when she's ticked off at the not-quite-a-demon guy."

Did these ladies know how to take no for an answer? If the gym thing was any indication, I was betting that was a negative. I didn't know how much of my life I wanted slipping into the pages of books that would go out to millions of people.

"I can see this worries you. Some people love the idea. I have an aunt who has to be the most boring person on the planet and yet she's always calling me to tell me something she thought was super funny to put in a book."

"I'm kind of boring." Or, I would be after this.

"No, you're really not. And you're the best kind of not boring. You don't go out looking for adventures. They just kind of fall in your lap."

"Yeah, this unemployed-slash-single-slash-homeless thing is working out really awesome." Note the sarcasm.

"What are you talking about? You got rid of a corporate noose. Dropped a guy you shouldn't have wasted time on. You're living in a gorgeous walk-up in one of the most beautiful neighborhoods in the country. Seriously, if I'd known Ben was just going to rent it out cheap, I would have told him I was homeless a month ago. Now you're running your own business and you're obviously talented. This month rocks." She glanced away and raised her mug to her lips. "Plus, you've got Mr. Law and Order on the string."

"I do not—You know what? Believe what you want. I'm too sore to argue about anything."

"How about this, I'll ask permission to use anything you say and we'll go case by case."

Did my life get weirder this week? I mean, before I just went to work, went home, had dinner, hung out with Jason, repeat. This was weird, right? Having people steal my name and my experiences to put in books and living in someone else's home? Not to mention I just went to the gym.

Going to the gym might be the weirdest part come to think about it.

"Okay. Case by case."

"Excellent." Hailey pulled a tiny notebook out of her bag. "I would officially like to put in a request to at some time use the break-up story including the post break-up tire situation in a story. Granted?"

"Sure. Why not."

She scribbled in the notebook and dated it before drawing a little line under it. "Initial here, please."

"Seriously?"

"Yes. And you can't give this story to Jenna now. I have dibs."

"My life is so not that interesting."

"You may be my new muse." She collapsed back in her chair as I made a show of initialing the page. "Best. Day. Ever."

My new friends were crazy.

TWENTY-ONE

STRANDED. SO CLOSE, and yet so far.

I closed my eyes and rested them against the lovely wrought iron work of the stoop's banister.

"Kasey?"

Oh, so not what I needed.

I glanced up to see Max standing there, looking annoyingly fit and not at all sore. I tried to ignore the little blue running shorts and white t-shirt with the words Police Academy sweat plastered across his annoyingly perfect chest.

"Max. Hey. What's up?"

"Just went for a run." He glanced down at the rolly cart with my groceries in it. "You?"

"Oh, you know."

"No. Not really." He glanced down at my groceries again and then studied my face. "Okay, bruiser. Where'd you get the black eye?"

He squatted down in front of me, turning my head with a soft touch to my chin to look at my bruise. He must have been really worried, because he wasn't inscrutable today.

"Oh, you know."

"Again, not really."

"Well, I went to the gym—"

"All I need to know is if I have to arrest someone or beat the crap out of them."

Well, that was oddly sweet.

"Not unless you have something against treadmills."

Max looked at me like I was insane—which he was probably building a pretty good case for at this point. Instead of having me institutionalized, he just shook his head and stood back up.

He glanced down at my cart. "Are you going somewhere?"

"Just enjoying the air."

"Really?"

"Yup."

"And, that ice cream I see sitting on top of your groceries...It's just catching some rays?"

I really had nothing to say to that. It was two days after I'd made the fatal error of going to the gym with Hailey and I think my body was boycotting life to pay me back. The first morning I'd been sore, but this morning I'd woken and barely been able to sit up to get out of bed.

Worst. Day. Ever.

I'd remembered what she'd said about walking. Maybe it would make me feel better. Only, now, with my groceries sitting at my feet, I couldn't get up the three-and-a-half flights of stairs to my apartment, let alone pick up four bags of groceries. My legs were being very clear that added weight would be rejected and my arms were letting them know that it didn't matter because they couldn't pick up a dead leaf let alone a gallon of milk.

Max looked me over and may have almost smiled. I think.

"A little sore?"

Knowing Max, there was no way out of this. I might as well just admit it.

"More than a little."

"Why don't I take those up for you?"

If I'd been able to move, I might have actually thrown my arms around him in gratitude.

See? One good thing about this inability to make my limbs move: No stupid moves either.

"That would be great." I handed him my keys and he used it as an opportunity to pull me to my feet before carrying the rolly cart from the sidewalk up to the front door. By the time I got there, he was holding the door open with the cart inside.

He picked the full cart up as if it weighed nothing and headed up the stairs at a brisk pace.

I remembered fondly the days when my body knew what a brisk pace was.

I listened to his footsteps pound their way up and then the snick of my door falling shut with a soft bang, then his steps coming back down the three flights of stairs. By that time, I hadn't even made it to the mid-way landing to the first floor.

He stood at the top, hands on his hips, looking like a clean cut, gym gladiator, judging me from the top of Mount Perfect Conditioning.

"This isn't going to work." He strode down the stairs to where I was, looking as determined as he always did. Then walked past me and turned around.

Dear Lord, please don't let him think pushing me up the stairs by my butt was a good idea. Not only had it become painfully—literally—obvious that my butt was not all I had hoped it was, but that was really going to hurt.

"Turn around." Ah, Max in his gentle way of making requests.

I turned around, having no idea what he had planned. He stepped up one more step, shoved his shoulder into my squishy midsection, and hefted me over his shoulder.

Then started climbing the first flight as if I were a very light sack of potatoes.

"Max," I gasped out his name, trying to catch a breath as I adjusted to let my lungs move. "Put me down."

"I'd rather not leave you sitting on a flight of stairs and wondering if you made it home tonight."

"Don't you have somewhere to be?"

"Nope. Worked a double yesterday."

"A date or something?"

"No date."

"It's a good night to call your mother."

"Speak with her every Sunday."

Of course he did. He probably had a checklist on his fridge. Things Every Annoyingly Good Guy Should Do.

We turned past the landing on the second floor. At this point, I was just counting the steps 'til my gut was no longer used as a pivot point. He'd kicked my door open before walking me over to the small kitchen island and putting me down next to one of the stools.

"Sit."

"Woof."

Max turned and gave me a look like I was speaking a different language. As if I really could speak Dog. I rolled my eyes because he brought out my inner teenager.

"Have a seat in your own home and make yourself comfortable, Kasey, would have been a slightly more reasonable way to boss me around."

He ran his hand through his wind-messed hair and gave it a tug.

"Kasey, if you wouldn't mind taking a seat, I'll put your ice cream away before it melts."

"I can put my own groceries away."

"Sit."

Well, the polite thing lasted about four seconds longer than I'd expected it to.

And yet, I sat. I was too tired for this. The sooner he put my groceries away, the sooner he'd be gone, and the sooner I could sink into my incredibly small, old building bathtub.

The first thing he did was put the ice cream and milk away, then he went to the sink, filled a glass with water and started opening and closing drawers. One drawer after another.

"Where's your ibuprofen?"

"In the bathroom."

"Stay."

I almost made the woof joke again, but I doubted it would have gone any better.

He came back and set the glass and pills in front of me before going back to unloading my grocery rolly cart. Soon a banana was placed before me.

"Potassium."

"Yellow."

"What?"

"I don't know. I thought we were naming obvious characteristics of things."

"No. Bananas have potassium which is good for the muscle soreness."

"Oh."

I was tempted to wait and see if the next command would be *eat*, but figured I was going to do it anyway so why give him the opportunity to be bossy.

"Thanks."

"You need me to peel that for you, Wonder Woman?"

"No. I think I've got it."

I bit in, watching him wander around my kitchen, more at home in it than I was yet. Before I knew what he was doing, he'd pulled out my cutting board.

"What are you doing?"

"Making stir fry."

Stir fry? I had stuff to make stir fry with? What was even in stir fry?

"Don't you have your own kitchen?"

"Yes. But if I go make stir fry there, it will be cold by the time I get back."

"Max, you can't just come into someone's house and start cooking."

"If I leave, what are you going to do?"

"Take a hot bath and then lie on my couch while wishing to die."

"Exactly. Why don't you go take a hot bath, then come out and eat stir fry? Then you can lie on your couch watching the new X-Men movie and wishing to die."

"I don't have the new X-Men movie."

"Yes, but I do. So you're all set." He turned back to the countertop and pulled out a skillet, obviously dismissing me in my own home.

Well, fine. If he wanted to play butler, I was going to go take a bath. It would serve him right. Cooking in some strange woman's house while she soaked in the tub. I locked the door behind me and turned the water on, looking for that perfect bubble bath heat level.

A rap-rap-rap sounded on the door. Seriously, my apartment was too small for him.

"Don't forget Epsom salt if you have any."

"I'm pretending you're not here!"

"Fine. Pretend I'm not here in Epsom salt."

"Fine." I mocked under my breath. "Pretend I'm not here."

"What?" His voice was farther away, probably in the kitchen.

"Nothing."

I started peeling off clothing and realized I was about to get naked with a man in my apartment. Yes, he was locked out of the room, but still. I hadn't gotten naked with anyone but Jason in years. Not that I would have been a random-naked-getter, but still.

It took me longer to pull my t-shirt off than I wanted. I would have liked to blame it on the guy in the next room making me nervous, but it was more that I couldn't lift my arms over my head.

Stupid arms.

Footsteps to the door. Pause. Rap-rap-rap.

"Kasey, I'll be right back."

"Yeah. Take your time."

The footsteps headed away and then the soft fall of the door echoed down the non-existent hall to me.

I settled into my bath *with* Epsom salt and tried to figure Max out. I'd never met anyone as bossy as him. Even Jason paled by comparison. Max with his, *sit-stay* routine was getting old. But, his direct approach at least lacked the manipulation Jason's control always had.

I was never a bath person, so after five minutes I was already bored and wondering what someone does sitting in tepid water waiting for it to get cold. Maybe if I'd brought a book in with me. I'd ordered Jenna and Hailey's first two books and was trying to figure out which one to start with, but unless I wrapped my phone in a Ziploc bag, there was no way I'd trust myself with it around water.

As boredom turned to mind-numbing boredom I got out of the tub and headed to my room before Max could get back. I thought about putting on something cute, but figured that it was his fault he was here. I was too sore to try to look nice and the last thing I needed was a man, so I grabbed my yoga pants and a Sox baby tee.

Oddly, I actually owned a yoga mat. I'd won it at the company picnic. It was soft and cushy and didn't let the ground's dampness soak through. This was what yoga mats were really invented for. I rolled it out in the living room and tried to work out some of my muscles. If I couldn't get in and out of my apartment on my own, I was afraid Max would keep stopping by to carry me around.

Just as I lay flat and stretched my arms up over my head, feeling my entire body expand, there came a knock at my door. Hopefully he was smart enough to have brought my keys.

"Come in?"

The door opened and Max came in carrying a grocery bag. He stopped just inside the door.

"Are you stuck?"

"No. I'm stretching."

He just stared at me, flat out on my floor.

"Are you sure?"

It took me a moment to realize this was a real question.

"Yes, I'm sure. I'm stretching."

"I thought you didn't stretch."

"Well, there's a day for everything. Obviously, I need to take better care of my body if you people are going to keep trying to kill it."

"Who else has tried to kill your body?"

"Some guy grabbed me and nearly had me vomit all over him running up three flights of stairs with my gut shoved into his shoulder."

"You're welcome." He grinned, that darn dimple peeking out, and headed toward the kitchen. Laying the grocery bag down, he started pulling food out of my fridge. Apparently he'd already rinsed stuff since it was all collected in a colander on a plate. Then tossed a DVD across the room onto the couch and got back to work.

I decided I would be forgiving and let him do whatever he wanted to in my kitchen. I was magnanimous that way. Rolling onto my side, I managed to get on my knees and push myself up using the coffee table.

"Need a hand?"

I glanced over my shoulder at Max, leaning against my counter with his arms crossed looking a bit smug.

"No. I'm good." I braced myself on the coffee table and used my arms and legs to get up. Slowly.

"Sure?"

"Yup. All set."

After the longest twenty seconds of my life, I was upright and ready to hobble across the room where I then had to lower myself onto a stool. None of that was comfortable or easy. A new appreciation for people with walkers imprinted itself on my soul.

He set all his ingredients out in a straight row, organized and in some Max pre-approved order, and began chopping peppers. It gave me a moment to study him, and I finally noticed through the haze of receding pain that he'd changed and his hair was damp.

"Did you shower?"

"Yup."

"That fast?"

"Yup."

"Shut up, Max. You're talking my ear off."

He grinned.

I ignore the dimple.

"I figured I'd start to stink eventually if I didn't. I did nine miles before carrying a sack of potatoes up three flights of stairs."

"Nine miles? What's with you people?" Maybe it was a cop thing with him. "Is it for your job?"

He shook his head and turned around to start the stove.

"I do feel more confident in my job if I'm fit, but I just like taking care of my body."

Without my permission my eyes took in that very fit body, drifting down his shoulders to his butt.

"Is there something on my ass?" Max asked, his gaze tracking mine from over his shoulder.

Um, jeans? Very perfectly fitting jeans.

"I thought so." I cleared my throat, hoping I'd stop squeaking. "But maybe it was just the light."

Max looked up at the recess lighting and that darn dimple snuck out. "Yeah, crazy light in here."

"So, nine miles. That's not something you do every day, is it?"

"Nope. Just when I have a day off. I only do two miles each morning when I get up for work."

"That's a sickness."

He laughed outright and it took me by surprise, the gut deep, rough sound of it.

"Yeah. I tried to get help. No one seemed to be able to break me of my don't get fat, stay healthy addiction. Real shame."

Well, when he put it like that I began to wonder what he and Hailey thought of me and my inability to do one day at the gym.

"Shawn was horrible."

"Shawn?"

"The trainer guy."

"Oh." He turned back and started dicing chicken. "He was a jerk?"

"Um, no. He was just..." With my luck, Shawn was Max's trainer too.

"Tough?"

"He made me run on a treadmill."

"Did you tell him you weren't a runner?"

"Um, so yeah. He told me to walk. But there were all these buttons." I waved a hand dismissively, as if the buttons couldn't be explained in the normal world.

"So, you just kept pressing buttons."

"Well, I mean, it's *walking*. I walk every day."

"Today being the exception."

"I walked today."

"Okay, today being the exception of you walking well." He winked at me and I tried to be annoyed with him, but it was slightly absurd. "So, you ran on a treadmill and that's why you're so sore?"

"Isn't that what people in your field call a leading question?"

"Just answer the question, Tuesday."

"Okay, so it wasn't just the running. Those things are deadly."

Max set the knife down and leaned toward me. "Please don't try to tell me that this somehow has to do with your black eye."

This conversation wasn't going the way I'd hoped. Shocker.

"It *threw* me against its dashboard thing and then spit me out against the wall. Those walls are hard."

"Cinderblocks usually are."

"And then there were squats. With weights. And crunches. And these things on this ginmorous ball that I couldn't stay on. And more weights. It felt like I was there for *hours.*"

I saw the darn dimple come out as he turned his back to me and asked, "How long were you there?"

"I guess about forty-five minutes."

"How much of that was on the attack treadmill?"

"Too much."

"Mmm-hm."

I wasn't sure what that meant, but I suspected it was his way of not having to say anything to avoid laughing at me. Which was fairly nice considering.

Max started doing something in one of my pans that smelled like heaven and I gave up caring what he thought about my workout inabilities and more about what he was going to feed me and why nothing I cooked in that pan ever smelled as good.

Figures he cooked.

"Do you have wine glasses?"

Because the old cabinets were old, small built-ins, they weren't tall enough for wine glasses, so I'd put those in the little space underneath my TV where other people probably stored movies and games. Ah, city living. After making my way across the room far more easily than earlier, I still had no interest in squatting down to get the glasses. Bending at the waist seemed like a far better option. I pulled out two glasses and made my way back to the stool where I probably should have asked for a cooking demonstration as he'd worked.

Max stood there, just shaking his head at me.

"What?"

"Nothing."

"That's not nothing."

"You just look…comfortable."

I had no idea what that was supposed to mean. Of course I looked comfortable. I was aiming for a night in on my couch. Just because Mr. I'm In Control had added himself to the agenda didn't mean I was going to dress up.

After a moment, he added, "Yoga pants."

"What? Do you have a thing for yoga pants?"

"Tuesday, all men have a thing for yoga pants. Especially when they fit like those."

With that, he turned back to the stove and started dishing out things into serving bowls while I pondered the show I'd just given him in my yoga pants and little t-shirt.

Not that it mattered.

He set a plate of stir fry and couscous in front of me and poured each of us a glass of wine before coming around and joining me at the counter.

"I hope you like it."

"It smells great. I'm sure I will." And then I bit into heaven.

This was just not fair.

"So, tell me something." I scooped more food into my mouth, not wanting to wait even knowing there were seconds waiting for me. "Tell me something you're really bad at."

"What?"

"Something you're bad at."

He set down his fork and turned his body to face me being all inscrutable again.

"Why?"

"Everything you do you seem to be good at. Are you good at everything or do you just not do things you're bad at?"

Max shifted back around and rested an elbow on the counter, looking off through my wall to who knows where and downed half a glass of wine.

"Apparently, I was horrible at being a boyfriend."

Well, that wasn't what I was expecting.

"What makes you say that?"

"Probably that my girlfriend slept with one of my coworkers."

I froze, the fork halfway to my mouth, at a loss of what to say. Sure, Jason had turned out to be a jackass, but I was pretty sure that while I dated him, he was one-hundred percent my jackass. Lucky me.

"Um…"

"Yeah. Pretty much the normal response."

He went back at his food with a new focus, but I couldn't let it go. He obviously hadn't. That bothered me more than I could say. That this guy I was pretty sure was a pain in the butt, but a completely honorable one, would feel bad about the actions of someone else.

"Were you mean to her?"

"What? No." He slammed the fork back down. "Of course not."

"You didn't cheat on her, I assume."

He didn't even bother to reply to that. Just gave me a look that answered that question and what he thought of it.

"Did you break promises?"

"Sometimes I was late because of work, but I always texted to let her know."

"Did you flirt with other women?"

He looked appalled, as if men didn't come on to women who weren't their girlfriends all the time.

"Why would I commit to someone if I wanted to be with other women?"

"If you could answer that question, we could solve half of the first world problems."

He pushed his food around his plate, slouching a bit in his chair which worried me more than the scowling. "She said we never talked and I didn't listen to her."

I sat there, trying to piece together this mystery that was Max. Obviously he wasn't a man who spoke a lot, but he did seem to listen, even if he barreled through and did what he wanted to anyway.

"Yeah, see. I can see that. You're agreeing with her." He shifted back around and picked up the bottle of wine, refilling his glass a bit more than the one before it.

"I'm not *agreeing* with her. But you do have a habit of just doing what you think is right whether people want you to or not."

"Oh, really? And you know this after only a week?" He crossed his arms and added, "Give me one example."

I raised an eyebrow at him and he mirrored it back, waiting for me to come up with *just* one example.

I pointed at my meal.

"Dinner? I made you dinner and that's your example of not listening to you?"

"You didn't say, *Hey. Kasey. I know you're in pain, how would you like me to throw together a little something?* You just started cooking in my kitchen even after I told you all I wanted was a bath and a movie."

"But you're getting a bath and a movie."

"On your terms."

"Sometimes people need to be taken care of."

The muscle at his jaw ticked and the fingers on my wine glass tightened.

"Yes," I answered, not sure of what else to say.

"And, sometimes it's nice to just do things for people. Especially if you're dating her."

"That's true."

"And you would assume that if two people were dating, making a meal one night when one person wasn't feeling well would be a good thing."

Well, I couldn't argue with that, except...

"We're not dating."

"I didn't say we were." He flashed me a grin, more cocky looking than before. "Are you hinting at something, Tuesday?"

Incorrigible. That's really all I could say about him.

"Nope."

"I'm just saying that," he went on innocently enough, "I need to be able to take care of people I care about. If she had a problem with it, she could have told me instead of inviting my friend over and greeting him at the door in her bra and underwear."

That was...Who does that? Who purposefully sets out to hurt someone that badly just because he was a little too much with the being-in-charge thing?

"I can't argue with that." Because, what sane person could?

"Thank you."

That was probably the best place to leave this conversation. I let Max put the dishes in the sink but told him he couldn't wash them. I could see the hesitation on his face, but he nodded and left them there. It was probably going to kill him before the night was over. But, in light of our earlier conversation, I was really impressed he allowed me to leave my own dirty dishes in my sink.

I wandered over to the small living room set Ben had left in my care and curled up in the corner. Max continued to make himself at home putting the movie in and walking around adjusting lights. It was hard to fault him when I was filled with great food and exactly where I wanted to be.

I expected him to take the chair in the corner. Instead he plopped down on the other end, grabbing the remote and hitting play as if we did this every weekend.

The movie flickered on and I got sucked into the world of good and evil and what would my super power be.

I was pretty sure Max really would be a super hero if they existed. Him and his keeping people safe, always being there thing.

I tried to stretch my legs out without kicking him, but failed miserably when my heel took him in the side.

"Kasey, just stretch out."

I felt odd putting my legs across him and looked at his lap as if it might be radioactive. Instead, I shifted to try to put them on the coffee table at his end.

"Unless..." He glanced at the blanket I was tucked under, lifting the edge and pretended to peer under. "Is it because your feet are naked? If it makes you feel more comfortable, I could get my feet naked too."

My gaze drifted over to where Max's sock covered feet were propped up on the table. He probably had really strong, not hairy, perfectly shaped feet. The kind of feet you see on the movie posters walking down the beach next to a set of dainty lady feet.

There was seriously something wrong with me.

"No. No, need to get your feet naked." I cleared my throat. "I just, you know, feel like it's weird to be using you as a footrest."

"It's not weird. Just stretch out. I don't care." He picked up my feet and pulled them onto his lap, sliding a little toward me so my feet hung over his far leg. "See, not weird."

I nodded, shifting my focus back to the movie and Hugh Jackman and trying ignore it as Max's handed rested across my calf.

I couldn't even enjoy the last fifteen minutes. I kept thinking about not moving my feet or my legs or wondering why his hand was on my calf. Was it because my calf was in his way or was he *touching* my leg, touching my leg?

As the credits rolled, I sat up, thinking about pulling my feet away, but before I could, he lifted them again, slid out from under them and headed toward the TV.

"That was better than I thought it would be. The trailer was kind of lame compared to the one last summer." He crouched in front of the TV set-up and ejected the DVD. "What did you think?"

I think I needed to get him out of my apartment. This was supposed to be a quiet night at home recovering from Hailey's abuse.

"Yeah. It was good. I liked the earlier ones better."

He glanced over his shoulder, giving me a look that obviously said my flat tone came across loud and clear. Instead of asking what had turned me into weird-o girl, he just nodded and starting putting everything away.

He headed toward the door, grabbing his corkscrew and sauté pan off the counter as he went.

"Come here and lock me out."

Oh, yeah.

I pulled myself off the couch, happy to see I was moving a little more easily and knowing there was no way I'd leave the house tomorrow.

At the front door, he half stepped into the hall before turning back to look at me.

I made the mistake of looking up at him. Jason had been a lot taller than me. He was a lean six-foot-one. But, Max at his more modest five-ten felt bigger as he filled my doorway, and closer. Amazing how much closer he felt with just a few inches of height lost.

He stood there, looking down at me and I felt the need to fill the silence with something for some reason. Unsure why or what, I finally landed on, "Thanks."

Max grinned and shook his head. "Sure. Don't forget the dishes."

And then, before you could say *apartment takeover*, he was gone.

TWENTY-TWO

MY BLARING ALARM clock sounded, pulling me out of another weird dream. More Max. More Max and kitten calendars. This calendar's year was all cooking. Eggs, steak, cupcakes, kebobs. If I would eat it, there was a month for it.

This time, Max stood in a gourmet kitchen, wearing jeans and an apron, his shoulders broadly outlined by the thin white straps. The kitten perched on his shoulder, a little chef's hat on his head, his tail gently wrapped around the back of Max's neck to drape down his shoulder.

I reached over and slammed the alarm clock off, happy to have my weird internal voice shut up.

Max.

I could lie to Jenna and Hailey, but I had to admit it to myself at least. I was attracted to Max. It wasn't even just the hot cop uniform. He was completely the opposite of what I wanted, and yet...

If I was going to get my life back on track, I needed to stay out of his sphere as much as possible. Too many women had been drawn by the siren's call of flat abs. I would not be wrecked on the shore of male beauty.

I looked around my new apartment and thought again about how free I felt out from under Jason's controlling shadow. Lying in bed, I listened to the birds outside my window shout at each other and made a mental list of my day.

Get up, get dressed, eat something. Those all seemed obtainable since my body was once again doing what my brain told it to.

I finished the mental checklist and decided it was early enough to head over to The Brew to get some work done. If I stayed in on a nice day like this, I'd just get cabin fever.

Luckily, there were only to-go regulars there grabbing their morning mixes when I set up. I would be distraction-free now that Jenna's office was repaired.

Hopefully she wouldn't totally forget about me without our shared workspace.

I powered up my laptop and set in to answering the emails I was getting. Still nothing big enough to think of as an actual job, but people were checking in and getting more information. Not bad for my first week in business.

I created a FAQ page for my website and a contact form for the inquiries I seemed to see the most. Then I finished the mock-up of Jenna's new landing page which turned out pretty kick-ass. Moving down the to-do list, I emailed The Village council to see if they needed any flyers made for their Farmers' Market and Sidewalk Sale day.

All in all, a pretty fine morning.

I was getting ready to take a break when Jenna wandered in, her nose in a little red notebook as she scribbled away. A kindly patron pulled a chair out of her way as she beelined for the sofas.

Dropping her laptop bag on the chair, she stood and continued writing until she was done.

I'd learned by example watching Ben to just let this play out and then talk. Anything said while a notebook was opened was not actually said.

Or, as Dane put it, if a friend speaks in the notebook void, does anyone hear them?

"Hey." She collapsed into her chair, a look of anguish on her face.

"What's wrong? Is Ben okay? Is anyone hurt?"

She looked at me, her eyes still damp from unshed tears and said, "Chloe is going to college and I don't know what I'm going to do."

"Chloe your…sister?"

Did Jenna say she had sisters? In my head she was an only child, but I'd been meeting so many people I could have gotten confused.

"No." Her lips quivered as if fighting not to smile and she slouched back in the chair. "You'll think I'm absurd. Even Ben occasionally thinks I'm absurd."

"I'm pretty sure Ben thinks you're adorable even when he thinks you're being absurd."

"But still…Chloe is the character of my series. I've been writing her since she got to high school. It's one of the longest running single author YA contemporary series currently. Thirteen books. And now, she's going to college and I have to let her go."

Okay, so that was a little...absurd.

But, I'm sure in her world it was totally normal. I mean, there are books I've read that I hated when they ended.

This was obviously killing her.

"Aren't you ready for a new adventure?" Because, New Adventure was my new middle name. Maybe I should hyphenate it. "Change can be good. You might have something really exciting in you that you couldn't see because it was standing behind Chloe and once you send her off to her new home, you'll be able to start on it."

Before the words were even all out of my mouth, tears were streaming down Jenna's face. She lifted a hand to cover her mouth and dropped her eyes shut.

Crud. I was really horrible at this girlfriend thing. I had no idea what I'd said to make her cry, but it was obviously the worst possible thing. She sat there, pulling in on herself while I glanced around the room desperately looking for a distraction.

"I'm sorry. Whatever it is I said, I'm really, *really* sorry."

I half jumped, half crawled over the coffee table between us and set my butt on it taking her free hand in mine.

"What is it? This can't be about your series ending, right?"

Writers weren't that crazy, were they?

I considered the tree in her office and the way she talked about Chloe's day as if it were real.

Okay, maybe they could be that crazy. But this didn't feel like that.

"People just...leave, you know? They're there and they're this huge part of your life, and then they just up and move across the ocean never to be seen from again."

Ah.

"I don't think you'll never hear from Ben again." I patted her knee, trying to get her attention.

"I meant," she sniffed, "you know, people *in general.*"

I was really rusty on my girl speak apparently because I was about one-thousand percent sure we were talking about Ben.

"You're talking about Ben." Yeah, smooth.

Jenna burst into tears again.

I glanced over her shoulder at John standing behind the counter looking panicked. No help there.

"I *am* talking about Ben," she sobbed as if she were revealing a big secret.

"Ben loves you. And, he's coming back. You're not going to never hear from him again."

"He asked me to go with him." The words burst out of her mouth so fast it was as if she'd been standing in front of them holding them back until her knees gave out from exhaustion.

"That doesn't sound like a man who's looking to toss you aside."

"I said no." She sniffed and shook her head as if she didn't understand it herself. "I said no."

I thought of Jenna and Ben and then I thought of Jason and it took everything in me to not scream, *Good Lord, woman! Why?*

Instead, I took a deep breath and asked it more softly and without the lord's-name-in-vain part.

"I don't know. I just, it seemed like so much. I followed my high school boyfriend to college and that turned out horrible. Like, left at the altar horrible. What if I followed Ben all the way to a different country and then he left me? I'd just be sitting on a rainy sidewalk in the middle of London almost getting hit by cars going the wrong direction."

I'll say this for her, the girl had a vivid imagination.

"I don't want to be the naysayer here, but I don't think Ben would just drop you and leave you to fend for yourself."

"That would be even worse. What if we got to London and he realized he attached himself to a goofy, introverted, awkward nerd and now as a cosmopolitan international lawyer fighting environmental bad guys he saw how mismatched we were and *didn't* dump me out of pity?"

"I think he already knows who you are." I pictured the look Ben gave Jenna when she was being particularly Jenna and smiled. The man loved that side of her. I imagine that compared to working with complex world issues all day, Jenna's feyness had to be a restful place for his soul.

"He can't possibly."

"If he really did see you that way, then he probably would have taken this assignment as a chance to see what being apart was like. He'd be all let's-take-a-break guy. He wouldn't be the guy asking you to go with him."

"He's very polite."

I snorted. Only Jenna could think someone would ask her to move across the world with him because he was being polite.

"No one is that polite." I waved my hand between us before she could tell me that Ben was. "Have you asked him?"

"Asked him what?"

"If he wants to take a break?"

She stared at me as if I'd told her to kill the darn dream kitten. Which—no. I wasn't that desperate.

Yet.

"What if he says yes? What if he wants to take a break?" I didn't blame her for the horror she felt at that thought. If I had a guy who I loved like she loved Ben, not to mention who looked at her the way he did, I'd be horrified at tempting the fates too.

"I'd bet everything I have that he wouldn't. I'd bet you'd actually scare the snot out of him and he'd think you were trying to dump him."

She pondered this. Any other woman would be using this as a test, as a weapon. But I knew Jenna. Part of her was considering it because if Ben would be happier without her, she'd let him go. She'd suffer and she'd enter that suffering with her eyes open, but she'd do what she thought was best for him.

"Maybe," she started as she raised her free hand to gnaw at her cuticles. "Maybe I'll wait until close to when he goes."

"Will you be all mopey-sad eyes until then?" I grabbed her hand and yanked it from her mouth in a sad attempt to rescue her knuckles.

She yanked it back and wiped her eyes, a new surety entering her gaze.

"No. No moping. If this is the end, I want to enjoy it all. I'll make sure we have the best two weeks ever."

She gave a sharp nod as if agreeing with her own statement and was forming a plan already. Jenna was sure she'd be creating memories that would have to last her a lifetime. I was sure she'd only be driving more desperation into Ben to keep her with him.

I kind of wish she'd taken my bet, I could use the money. I was that sure of him.

"Thanks, Kasey. You're a really good friend. I don't know what I'd do if you hadn't been here for me."

She patted my hand as I let hers go and rose to head toward the counter as if everything that had just happened had been neatly put in a box to store for later. I knew that box would be forgotten in some mental storage unit, but I was glad she was able to do it.

I watched her, shocked at how good it felt. I had actual friends. Or, at least one. Someone to do more than go out for a drink with after work. Someone who shared her problems with you and talked them through. Someone who trusted me to be honest with her and help where I could. I was enjoying that simple pleasure when a deep voice came from behind me.

"Hey."

I half expected see a kitten on Max's shoulder when I looked up at him.

Instead, he stood there in his cop gear, the memory of the night we met rushing up and over me like a wave on a flat ocean. Part of it was the hurt of standing on the side of the road in the dark, trying to figure out how my life had become so empty while Jason stood next to his car raving at me. But part of it was the look of disgust Officer Max had given him and the teasing *behave* he'd thrown at me.

"Hey."

He glanced toward Jenna at the counter before stepping around my junk to sit next to me. It was a relief to not have him hovering there, overwhelming me. Until I looked at him and realized he had the capacity to be overwhelming even if you put him in a well and had to shout down at him.

"What was that?" He angled his head at Jenna.

"What?"

"The breakdown."

Oh. I'd assumed he'd just gotten there.

"She's…" I didn't think sharing how Jenna was feeling with anyone was a good idea. Especially Ben's best friend. But, this group seemed really tight. I wasn't used to the politics of close friends. Not since undergrad. And my group had been all women then.

"She's…" Max looked at me then glanced her way and stole her seat. "She's worried that Ben doesn't want her to go to England even though he's bought her an open-ended ticket she can use any time and done everything but ask her to marry him because he's afraid that would just put too much pressure on her to do something she doesn't want."

How was I supposed to respond to that?

"Is that a question?"

"No. I wouldn't put you on the spot like that."

"Oh. Thank you." That was sweet.

No. Not sweet. Officer Max was not sweet…sans kittens.

"You know, they do that whole couple's rule thing, but he hasn't told her all that."

"Couple's rule?"

"You know. The no secrets thing."

"You mean they tell each other *everything?*" That meant anything one person figured out would go through the group twice as quickly.

He shrugged. "Sure."

Well, was that what he meant or not?

"Why doesn't he just tell her all this?"

Max leaned back and crossed one leg over the other, dropping his ankle over his knee. "Are we a couple?"

I tried to hide my panic.

From the way he rolled his eyes at me, I was unsuccessful.

Before I could blurt out a more polite version of, *No!*, Max shook his head and answered, "Then we don't have the couple's rule thing and I can't tell you."

I narrowed my eyes, trying to stare him down like he did to everyone else. Trying to get him to break.

Instead, he laughed at me.

"Tuesday, you're adorable. Never give that up."

I gave up.

Abby appeared in front of us, a to-go cup in her hand. "Max."

"Abigail."

"John wanted you to have your caffeine before you went all Berserker on him."

"Yes, I can see that you'd feel in danger of that."

Abby rolled her eyes like a pro, set the cup down, and wandered off.

Max took a deep drink from the cup, his eyes dropping shut. "I love that kid."

"For real?"

"Yup."

Who would have guessed it? Abby had a fan.

I glanced down at my computer where the screen had gone black, wondering what time it was and how long Jenna would hang out at the counter. Didn't Max have places to be? There was crime out there waiting to be fought.

But, safe crime. The type where no one shoots at him.

"No one shoots at you, right?"

"You mean, on a regular basis?"

Not the most comforting answer.

I closed my eyes and pictured him and kittens.

"What's that?" Suspicion actually crept into his voice like it was a real thing that could creep places.

"What?"

"That smile you just got." He set his cup down and turned to face me. "Are you *hoping* people shoot at me?"

"No." My voice shot over the café, ricocheting and bringing everyone's gazes back to me. "Of course not. Why would I hope that?"

"If I could figure out why you do the things you do, I'd probably win a Nobel."

"I'm not even going to reply to that."

He gave me a grin that said, *you just did*, and I forced myself not to reply to that.

"What do you want to do tonight?" He asked as he pushed himself out of the chair.

I glanced up from my chair at Max hovering, his to-go cup blocking a good look at him.

"Tonight?"

"Yeah. The part of the day when the sun is no longer in the sky."

"Did we have plans for tonight?" I glance toward Jenna wondering if I'd done something to be on the outs. If I'd already run through my welcome and was no longer the rookie member of the group.

"No. But I thought we could."

"Could what?"

It wasn't that I was an idiot, but I couldn't follow his logic at this point.

"Do something. I thought you and I could do something."

"So, instead of asking me if I *want* to do something you ask me *what* it is I want to do?"

"I planned to skip most of this conversation." He took a sip of his coffee. "Apparently I was wrong."

"You're wrong more often than you think."

He shot me a grin, dropping the coffee cup low enough that he made sure I could see that dimple. I was onto him. At some point a woman must have told him it was deadly. "I'm okay with that."

"Really? You don't seem like the type of guy who likes to be wrong."

"Actually, I just figured you were wrong about me being wrong, but I didn't want to get even more sidetracked."

That sounded more like Max.

"Right, so you're wrong and I'm going to be the bigger person." I gave him a smile and let him deal with that.

"What am I wrong about?"

Crud, I'd totally lost the thread of this conversation. It seemed to be pushing it to say *everything*. So, I fell back on an old reliable. "You know what you're wrong about."

Max laughed, a deep, startled sound that seemed to rise up from his chest and surprise him.

"Sure. Of course. So, tonight. What do you want to do?"

"You mean like a date?"

Max rolled his head, his gaze straying heavenward and I swear his lips moved, probably asking for patience or strength or understanding...but most likely for all of the above.

"How about just two people who have already enjoyed dinner and a movie and a foreign film and a coffee and a game night—"

"You enjoyed game night?"

He grinned, a wicked surprise of a grin I hadn't expected from him. "Yes."

I waited for him to elaborate, but that seemed to be a lost cause.

"So, tonight is just to hang out?"

"We'll hang out."

We stared at each others, both of us with narrowed gazes trying to read the other.

"Fine. I'd like to hear some live music."

"Really?" Now Max was the surprised one.

"Yes. I think I'd like it."

It was on The List I was informally making in my head of things single girls in the city did when not being distracted by a controlling boyfriend.

"Anything in particular?"

"Just nothing heavy-metal-ish."

"I'll pick you up at eight."

"I'll meet you on your stoop."

"How about I meet you on *your* stoop?"

"How about I decide where I meet you and text you tomorrow."

"For tonight?"

I gave him *my* The Look.

"Fine." Max downed the rest of his coffee, tossed the cup in the recycle bin, and pulled his little cop hat on. "Eight o'clock on my stoop."

Win!

"Stay out of trouble, Tuesday."

And off he went.

Jenna, conveniently was done with whatever she was doing at the counter and wandered over just then.

"Did he call you Tuesday?"
So much for staying out of his sphere.

TWENTY-THREE

I LEFT MY HOUSE absurdly early to walk the three-quarters block to Max's stoop. I had a completely rational fear that if I left on time he'd be standing at my door waiting for me.

He couldn't be trusted.

On the downside, between my making sure this wasn't a date and not asking him where we were going, I had no idea what to wear. My bedroom could now pass for a scene out of Law & Order. In cop lingo, it looked like it had been *tossed*.

I definitely needed to ask Max if cops really talked like that.

After trying on everything I owned more than once, I settled on skinny jeans, my most comfortable black heels, and a little black top that could go either way depending on location and accessories.

I'd never worn this outfit before. I checked myself out in the mirror a bit surprised. The skinny jeans were just nice enough to be saved for a night out and the top I'd only worn under little jackets at work.

More proof I was getting my life on the right track.

Also, if I was going to be honest, I looked super cute. Either that or I'd gone blind in exchange for a pretty decent ego boost.

Which meant that maybe I should change again. If I looked too cute then that might go against the whole not-a-date message.

But, Max agreed it wasn't a date. I think. Or he just agreed that he knew I didn't think it was a date. But, that would mean it's not a date. Something can't be a date if both people don't agree, right?

Crud. I should change.

Except, it was ten of eight and Max was probably plotting to beat me to my stoop before I could get to his.

I was going to have to head out in date clothes.

It was a risk I was willing to take.

I grabbed a light jacket and rushed down the stairs. Or, I rushed down two stairs, realized that rushing in non-work heels was almost impossible, pictured myself lying broken at the bottom of the first flight with Max shaking his head at me, and slowed down.

Glancing at the time on my phone, I considered sliding down the banister, but vetoed that as well.

At the front door, I glanced through the glass panes half-expecting him to be there.

When he wasn't, I fought off the tiny bit of disappointment I felt. I'd thought he'd be there. That's all. I wanted to be able to give him the not-a-date talk one more time and figured if he ignored my request that would give me an excuse.

An excuse to what? I'm not sure.

Instead, as I walked down the street, I could see him leaning against the banister at the bottom of his stoop, playing on his phone. He wore jeans that were just fitted enough to look good with a white button down shirt tucked in, the sleeves rolled up over his forearms.

I studied *his* outfit trying to figure out if he was wearing date clothes. He looked really good, but I didn't think that was the clothing's fault.

As if he had some type of radar, he glanced up and straightened as I made my way to him, the clicking of my heels the only giveaway someone was approaching. I tried not to blush as his gaze slid over me taking in my little shirt, fitted jeans, and peek-a-boo patent leather shoes. When he smiled that cocky smile I *knew* he thought these were date clothes.

Darn it.

"These aren't date clothes."

"Of course not."

I waited for the punch line, but when he didn't say anything else I had to bite my tongue from saying, *No really. They aren't.*

"You look very nice," was what he said instead.

"So do you."

"Thank you. I did something special with my hair."

I glanced up at his close cut hair, the top just long enough to not look military, trying to figure out what exactly that was.

"Tuesday, I'm kidding."

He took the last step down to the sidewalk and glanced at my shoes.

"How comfortable are those?"

"Very."

"So, if I said we were going to walk down to the waterfront and back tonight, you'd be okay?"

"Actually, yes. They're Franco Sarto."

"Whatever that means." He motioned for me to turn back the way I'd come and fell in next to me.

I glanced at my apartment as we went by realizing he hadn't pushed to pick me up even though it was the right direction. He'd understood it was important to me and didn't push.

"Thank you." I didn't even know I was going to say it until it was out of my mouth.

"For what?"

I studied the cracks in the sidewalk, making sure my heel didn't get caught in one...or my gaze in his. "For getting me out of the house tonight."

"Mmm-hm."

I was just going to pretend he believed me.

"Where are we going?" I asked, since it obviously wasn't the waterfront which was the opposite direction.

"It's a surprise."

I was about to tell him I didn't like surprises, but then realized I wasn't sure that was true. I didn't like surprises at work. I certainly didn't like surprise breakups that left me homeless. But maybe normal surprises were okay.

"Okay."

"Really?" Now *he* sounded surprised.

"I think so."

I walked on, considering I had so much to learn about myself. It was an almost frightening idea. It was like being a freshman in college all over again, but everyone else already had asked themselves these simple little questions.

I was a freshman at life.

Two blocks past my apartment, Max turned down a side street and crossed us out of our neighborhood toward one of the colleges. The beautiful oak trees stopped lining the road and the quaint lights turned into normal streetlights. After another two blocks, he motioned toward a building with a sign in Spanish.

"We're here." He pulled open the door, and heat and spices and music rushed over me like he'd opened a portal to another world. "I hope you like to salsa."

Salsa? I had a sick, sad feeling he wasn't talking about chips.

Inside the door, the bouncer stamped Max's hand and asked to see my ID. I pulled it out of the tiny wallet I'd stuck in my back pocket and waited while he stamped a blue star on my hand.

Max glanced over the heads of the girls standing in our way before he took my hand and pulled me through the crowd to the far end of the room. The music was quieter in the corner, but he still needed to speak up to be heard.

As we neared, a short man with two earrings in each ear spotted us and opened his arms as if he was going to hug Max. He came forward, his gaze dropping to where Max's hand was wrapped around mine.

"Maximo! You're here to dance with your lady."

His lady?

"Jorgie, this is my friend, Kasey." He beat me to the punch. "We're just here for the music tonight."

"No, no, no. You must dance. Everyone who comes in must enjoy the music on the floor. I will get you special song played later. Something easy to move to, si? Your lady has hips to move I see, no?"

Max glanced down at my hips, his lips quirked up on one side. Luckily he realized there was no right answer to that question.

"Just to listen. Julian Delgado is playing tonight, right?"

"Si, si. You never sit when they play. You'll be out there." Jorgie winked at me and headed toward the bar, pointing one of the waitresses our way.

"What would you like to drink?"

"You don't—"

"I know. I don't have to buy. But, here's the deal. Tonight is on me. If you want to do something some other time, I'll let you take me out. But there's a difference between being independent and being a pain in the ass. Now," he threw his arm around the back of my chair and leaned in, "stop being a difficult person to be around. What do you want to drink?"

I knew what he was saying. I hated that person, the one who made everything difficult. I guess finding the line between independence and pest was going to be harder than I thought. I was already trying to figure out where I'd want to take Max out when I realized he'd just tricked me into another night out. Maybe I'd treat him to an afternoon volunteering at a homeless shelter.

Of course, he probably already did that.

"Quit over-thinking, Tuesday. It's just a drink."

"Right." I glanced around at the atmosphere and the dancers and the light-wood bar on the far side of the room. "Sangria. This seems like a Sangria night."

"Is this another test or do you like Sangria?"

"I've had it before." Once. In undergrad. In Mexico. I'm sure it was totally going to be the same.

Max waved the waitress over and ordered a Corona and Sangria before leaning back in.

"Latón de Delgado is a favorite. You're going to love them." He grinned, that darn dimple peeking out. "They have lots of flavor."

I don't think I'd ever heard a band with flavor. It made me think of those scratch and sniff stickers from when I was a kid. Was there such a thing as listen and lick?

Okay, that just sounded gross.

On the stage, a group of men in black suits began setting up. Up front, a couple led a group of about fifteen people in what looked like a basic lesson. I watched, wondering if I should be up there learning. Was this something I'd enjoy? Had I been missing out on this?

"Do you want to go take the class?"

I turned my head, expecting Max to be over in his chair, but somehow he'd moved closer. Right next to me. I'd already been rethinking the dance lesson when I remembered I was completely uncoordinated and Max had already seen that in action...and my nearly naked butt in the process.

I glanced back toward where guys led the women across their bodies and into what looked like a very smooth turn. I imagined myself trying to walk past a guy that closely without falling over his foot, raising my arm past his face without breaking his nose, and walking under his arm without sticking my face in his armpit. "Um, maybe...not."

"Come on, Tuesday." He leaned in further, speaking right into my ear. "You're not afraid, are you? I won't let you do anything embarrassing."

I was trying to decide if that was better or worse than taking the lesson alone. Before I could come up with a snappy comeback—which with my luck would have happened next week—the music switched off and a man on the stage tapped the mic.

"Good evening, ladies and gentlemen. We're Latón de Delgado." And with that, he nodded once and the music came on live and loud. The floor was packed before the first line ended.

I watched, fascinated while the waitress laid our drinks out on the table and chatted with Max. I glanced up in time to see her lean far enough over to make sure he could confirm the color of the bra she was wearing as she thanked him for the tip. Max smiled at her, no dimple, and turned back toward me.

I quirked an eyebrow at him and grinned as the color rushed up his neck. For once he had no stoic look. He just turned back toward the dancers. His free hand rested on the table, the lead finger tapping in time to the music, his shoulders occasionally doing a little side to side like he was out there leading some girl around the floor. You could tell he loved this. I'd hate for him to miss the fun because I didn't dance.

"You can go dance."

Max shifted to look at me, his brows pulled down in what I'd finally figured out was a question.

"Dance." I pointed at the floor. "You can go dance if you want."

He shook his head, and shifted back around. I went back to watching the couples, amazed at how well some of them moved together, as if they could read each other's minds. Beside me, Max was all but dancing in his chair. Somehow, while being completely still, he was vibrating off energy to the music.

After two songs, the singer brought it back down and was speaking to the audience in Spanish.

"Do you want another drink?"

I glanced at my half-full Sangria. It wasn't my thing, but I was enjoying the change.

"No thanks. I'm still good."

I watched Max make his way to the bar. I watched other women watch Max make his way to the bar.

With a fresh eye, I studied him. He wasn't as good-looking as a lot of guys in the room. He wasn't pretty or handsome. He wasn't really rugged. All those catch words people used to describe heroes didn't fit him. He looked confident. He looked strong. His looks were classic without falling over into the category of a Kennedy or George Clooney. He was all clean lines and strong jaw and unreadable dark eyes.

But, when he moved…He moved like a man sure of his place in the world. A man who knew he could handle anything that came his way. And, unfortunately, he had the body to back it up. That lean, compact strength folded under those wide, powerful shoulders. No wonder we were all looking.

A woman pushed her way through the crowd to meet him at the bar, slowing her step to time it so she got there just in time. I watched as he smiled at her and she laid a hand on his arm. They chatted and she made a motion toward the dance floor.

It was about that time my fingernails were beginning to make little dents in my palms where my fists were clenched. I loosened them up, trying to shake my hands out without making it obvious.

Max wasn't mine. I didn't want him to be. Because, if he was mine then I was his. And, I wasn't ready to belong to anyone again. Max couldn't even handle letting me make my own dinner when I didn't feel well. I doubted if we were dating that he'd be able to deal with boundaries.

Not that I was considering dating Max.

Also, Max seemed to think I was nuts, so even if I did want to date him I was pretty much out of luck since he didn't seem like the kind of guy to go looking for a girl with the character trait of *crazy-pants*. So, it was totally a good thing that I wasn't considering dating Max.

And everything would just be fine if that girl in the super short skirt would take her hand off his arm.

Max shook his head and pointed back toward the table, obviously telling the hot, short-skirted girl that he couldn't go out on the floor and dance the sexy dance with her because he had to babysit the crazy pants at his table.

This was humiliating.

Max pulled his wallet out and paid for the drinks, grabbing them and giving the girl a smile as he headed back.

Well, this was going to be awkward.

Another song ended just as he dropped down into his chair.

"Are you having a good time?"

I was. I was totally having fun. I loved the music and was awed by the couples on the floor. The moves were gorgeous and sexy while still being fun and spontaneous. And, I liked being there with Max. It wasn't lost on me that he was nodding off girls who glanced his way who he probably danced with all the time. That he'd blown off hot, flippy skirt girl at the bar. That he'd come back to sit with me.

"I am, but…" The guilt started to punch at me about him sitting with me all night. "Why don't you dance? I mean, I can totally just hang out here and listen to the music for a bit while you get out there."

"I didn't come to dance."

My gaze slipped back to him and I couldn't help but feel the intensity of his focus.

I tried to see him outside of the light of Jason and his circle of fans. I studied him, studied the set of him and what I knew about him and tried to add it all up into something whole that I may have not seen—or ignored. How was I supposed to know? How could I judge if he was just another guy who was controlling and manipulative? Where was the line between controlling and being just a take-charge guy who wanted the best for me? Would a take charge guy know when to let me be in charge? Would it be a constant struggle? Would I ever—

"What?" Max asked interrupting my disturbing thought process.

"Nothing. I was just thinking." I tried not to blush, tried not to look at him any differently than I had a moment ago.

But, Max being Max he could probably read my mind. Or at least guess what I was thinking, because, as the band took the stage again, he winked at me before dropping his arm across the back of my chair and turning back to the dance floor.

The music came back up as couples filled the floor. A petite woman wove through the crowd, waving at Max before she even got to us. Max stood, stooping to kiss her on the cheek, obvious affection between them, but no chemistry.

I was glad because I'm not sure my nails would withstand another round of trying to split my palms open again. Not to mention that I was annoyed and confused enough.

Max introduced Eva and she started talking a mile a minute about learning salsa and meringue and how Max was one of the more patient guys who could actually dance and something about a cross body lead. It was clear she was hoping to get him out on the floor and was afraid to ask with me there, that she couldn't figure out what was going on between us.

I almost told her to join the club.

"Why don't you guys practice that move?" I suggested and grinned as the younger woman all but bounced on her toes.

Max looked down at me next to him, another one of his unreadable looks as he studied me.

"You wouldn't mind?"

"No. Of course not." And found I really didn't. Eva was sweet and obviously thoughtful considering she didn't try to seduce my date—*non*-date—out from under me. "It sounds like Eva's been waiting all week to see if she's nailed this move."

I looked up at him, trying not to notice how dark his eyes were and how intensely they studied me before that dimple broke out again.

"You're something else, Tuesday."

Before I could figure out what that meant, he offered Eva his hand and led her out onto the floor. They stayed at the edge, a more than comfortable distance between them, as Max patiently led her back and forth on the floor, every once in a while doing something with his hand that pulled her across the front of him and turned her about. Then back to the back and forth steps. One-two-three. One-two-three.

Compared to some of the overtly sexual dancing going on behind them, their little spins seemed almost sweet, with Max correcting her and letting her try again. After they'd done that a few times, he did some fancy thing where she spun half way around and did a little kick before coming back.

When the song came to an end, they both clapped politely before Max's hand dropped to her waist to guide her back to our table.

It was, unfortunately, one of the cutest things I'd ever seen. It was kitten worthy.

I was one cute thing away from insomnia.

Eva was talking a mile a minute when they got back, but she turned to me and thanked me for letting her use Max for practice, before taking off into the crowd again.

Max settled into the chair, a bit pink around the ears at the obvious adoration.

"You should have her hang out with Abby." I knocked his shoulder to get his attention. "Maybe they'd cancel each other out a bit."

"At seventeen, Abby's probably about thirty-seven years older than Eva."

I laughed because it was probably true, but also because I was suddenly nervous. I wasn't sure what to do about the fact that I was wearing date clothes on what felt like it was a date with a guy I swore I wasn't going to date but couldn't seem to stay away from.

Max leaned in, really leaned in this time. And, not as if he were just going to say something and it was loud. I fought to keep my gaze from dropping to his lips, but my eyes seemed to have a mind of their own. I wasn't sure what I'd do if he tried to kiss me. There was something about Max that pulled you in, but I hadn't wanted to *find* anyone.

I wanted to find *me*.

I was feeling more lost by the moment.

"Max."

It took me a moment to drag my gaze off him to the woman standing over us. Max's focus stayed on me, blocking her out. But, she obviously wasn't going anywhere. At some point, Max's hand had landed on my knee, drawing us together, connecting us. He gave my knee a little squeeze and turned to look up at the woman who still hadn't gotten the hint and gone away.

As soon as that focus was off me, I could breathe again.

I could also panic again.

Everything was shifting and I wasn't sure what to do.

"Olivia." Max sounded annoyed. It wasn't a normal sound for him and it made me pause, pulled me back outside of myself and my anxiety.

"You promised me a dance next time you were in." Olivia lifted her hand to her hip, turning sideways in her little flippy skirt as if she were on a fashion shoot.

"I'm here with someone." Max lifted his arm and let it settle across the back of my chair, leaning into me, his warmth seeping into me even with the heat of the club.

"You danced with Eva."

"Yes. I did."

I watched the interplay, wondering what my role in it was supposed to be, but suddenly feeling like I needed some time away from him. That some distance would definitely give me the perspective I was rapidly losing.

"You know what?" I stood and looked between them. "I have to run to the ladies room. I'll be back in a few minutes."

Max stared at me as if I'd abandoned him to hordes of angry zombies.

I felt a stab of guilt, but I hadn't told him to dance with her. I hadn't given her permission to dance with him—as if I had the power or right to do that. I'd just...abstained.

And escaped.

I definitely escaped.

I pushed my way through the overheated crowd almost rushing to where the ladies room sign glowed on the far side of the stage. Once I got to every woman's hideout, I shut the door behind me and splashed water on my face wondering where this night had gone so wrong.

Probably the date clothes. They were the reason everything felt so up in the air.

Just like Jason had taught me to dress for the job I wanted, I'd accidentally dressed for the man I was out with. I had to get myself under control.

I couldn't deny I was attracted to Max—more than that, I was drawn to him.

That was the most frightening part. If I had this draw, if I was pulled toward him, could I trust myself to know if he was safe? He got extra safety points for Jenna and Hailey both vouching for him. Ben seemed like a solid guy, so there was one more. And Dane—okay, maybe not Dane. Who knew what that guy thought was a trustworthy man?

Luckily, I didn't need to make a decision tonight. I just needed to enjoy myself.

I came out of the ladies room and glanced across the room to see if Max was still fighting off Olivia. Instead, I found them fairly quickly on the dance floor, her all but wrapped around him, the heat of the dance so fiery I could feel it from where I stood.

So, I did what any insane woman would do. I headed for the bar.

With the majority of people on the dance floor, it was easy to get the bartender's attention. "Hey, sweetness. What can I get you tonight?"

"I don't know. Something sweet and not too strong."

"Sure thing." He went to the far end of the bar and poured something from a pitcher into a little glass. "Here you go. It's a fruit sip."

Well, that sounded good. I took a sniff of sweetness before taking a sip. It tasted like pineapple and flowers. Which, hello. Why had I never heard of these fruity sipper things before?

I leaned against the bar and watched the all-kinds-of sultriness going on. From a distance it looked like Olivia was basically trying to climb Max. I wondered if she'd start pulling at his clothes in another minute. Max, leading Olivia and scowling at her. Of course, if Max was interested in me, scowling didn't necessarily mean anything bad. It could be how he looked at women he was attracted to.

I finished my drink more quickly than I meant to, arguing with myself the entire time. Annoyed Max was dancing with the hot girl. Annoyed he was dancing all the sexy-time dancing with her. Annoyed he'd said yes when I suddenly realized I'd wanted him to say no. Annoyed I was annoyed at all this.

I put my empty glass down and was turning away from the bar when the bartender handed me another one.

"On the house. You look like you need it." He set down another sipper in a slightly bigger glass and nodded his head toward Max and Olivia. "She's…Yeah, don't let her step between you guys again if you want to have a man when you leave tonight."

Great.

I wandered back to our table, trying not to watch them but morbidly fascinated. I studied their moves trying to figure out if Max was into her or was just going through the motions. Telling myself it didn't matter. Drinking my drink and hoping a happy little buzz would make sure it didn't.

I sat down, almost missing my seat, wondering if maybe that third-and-a-half drink wasn't the best idea.

But, of all the bad ideas I'd had tonight, it wasn't even in the top three.

Max spun Olivia out, stepping to the side when she came back. He really was smooth. Most guys used that to get closer to a girl, but he seemed to be using all his moves to keep some distance. I caught him once glancing over at me when Olivia basically tried to grab every part of him at once.

As soon as the music ended, Max stepped away, gave her a tight smile, and turned to work his way back to me.

At the table, he stood, gazed out over the crowd watching the band pushing into the next song. He lifted the nearly empty Corona to his lips and finished it off.

"You ready to go?"

I studied him, trying to figure out what that meant. Was he really done with the little club, was he done with Olivia, was he done with me? I pictured a long, silent walk home. But, in the end, it was getting late and I wasn't sure I wanted to watch another show quite like that one while I figured out what was going on in my head.

I stood, catching myself on the edge of the table as those drinks hit me. Isn't that always the way? You never know how much you've drunk until you stood up. And then—look out equilibrium!

I'd never been much of a drinker, so the floor moving seemed a little more suspicious than normal.

Not that the floor normally shifted.

Max grabbed me by the elbow, steadying me. "How much did you have to drink?"

"Just these two little things."

"Shots?"

"No. He said they were fruity sipper things."

Max rolled his eyes and mumbled under his breath about talking to Johnny. "Alright, Tuesday. Let's see if we can get you home without incident. You're light, but I don't think I can carry you that far."

Ha! I wasn't light. Jenna was light. Hailey was fit. I was all curvy squishiness. I studied his shoulders and reached out putting a hand on his chest to make sure it was as solid as it looked. "No. I think you could."

Max's hand came up and covered mine where it was over his heart, his gaze as deep and unreadable as ever. We stood there, me wondering if I'd ever know what he was thinking, until he smiled. It was a deep, full thing that crinkled the edges of his eyes and made that tight, sharp jaw relax.

He wrapped his hand around mine and shifted to start us through the crowd through the door.

"Here." Max held my sweater out for me to wrap myself in and, before I knew it, had taken my hand again, slowly leading us down the sidewalk.

I held on to him, enjoying the feel of my hand wrapped in his. The warmth and comfort and feeling of safety I got from knowing that I wouldn't fall.

Of just knowing that Max was there. That Max was with me.

I pushed the panic off and, for once, just let myself soak in his steady, sweet presence.

TWENTY–FOUR

WE GOT TO MY DOOR and I wasn't stupid enough to demand to walk Max back to his. That extra sixty feet seemed really, *really* far. I leaned forward, trying to see it through the parked cars.

"You're a ridiculous drunk."

"I'm not drunk." Was there something between pleasantly buzzed and drunk? "Well, not on purpose."

"Alright, Tuesday. Up you go." He nudged me toward my door and took my keys from me when I started fiddling with them. "Three flights and you can collapse into bed."

Bed sounded great. I was tired and just sober enough to realize that tonight hadn't gone at all like I'd expected it to.

I totally blamed the date clothes.

I headed in and wandered up the stairs knowing there was no sense arguing with Max on this one. The revelation about his ex and his desire to do things for people he cared about pounded heavier than my footsteps.

I couldn't help but wonder what was going to happen when we reached my door...well, my other door. I glanced at Max, my gaze dropping to his lips again. I'd heard the word chiseled used to describe men before, but everything about Max fit that: His jaw, his lips, his abs...the hard way he often looked at me.

"Face forward." His hand came up to rest on my lower back, probably to catch me when I went tips-over-toes back down the stairs. "You're halfway there."

Right. Stairs.

We rounded the top corner and stopped at my door. I leaned against the wall while Max unlocked it.

"You going to be okay?"

I nodded, trying not to stare at him again, wondering when I'd become so attracted to him.

"Right." He handed me my keys, gazing down at me as if he were going to say something more, which would have been really helpful to me right then.

Instead, he grinned that small grin, the one that just barely brought out his dimple and shook his head as if he were laughing at me. Or maybe himself.

"Night, Tuesday." He leaned down and brushed a kiss so quick I questioned it across my lips.

Before I could even contemplate if I wanted Max kissing me, he was gone.

TWENTY–FIVE

A T THIS POINT, the dancing kittens didn't even
surprise me.
Wake me up in a cold, romance-fearing panic?
Yes.
Surprise me? No.

TWENTY-SIX

I LAID IN BED trying to figure out who to call. I had more than Jayne now, but at the same time, every woman in my life had pretty much married me off to Max before he'd stopped scowling at me 100% of the time. I'd say 80% was a huge improvement. If I called Jenna or Hailey, they'd give me a long and detailed reasoning of why Max was the best guy in the world even though neither of them were dating him. Plus, they write romance'y fiction. How trustworthy were they really on this front. The whole hearts and flowers thing was part of their job description.

If I called Jayne, she'd suggest getting him out of my system. You'd think the girl slept with every guy she walked past the way she pushed me to hop into bed with him. She'd always been a relationship girl. Maybe this was whatever she was going through coming out vicariously.

And that was my fear—well, my additional fear. Beyond the one about falling in with another guy who would keep me in the box he used to define me and losing myself again. I feared that there was no getting Max Darby out of my system.

So, I called the only woman I knew who might offer another view.

"Hello?" The voice on the other end of the phone was as familiar as my own.

"Hi, Mom. How are you?"

"Kasey, honey, it's eight in the morning. Is everything okay?" Of course she'd start with that. Even though the woman gets up at six am every day.

"Yup. Just laying in bed about to start my day and thinking about you."

"Really?" She sounded suspicious. Of course, two calls to my mother in one month was highly unusual. But, oddly, the last one hadn't been as negative as usual. She hadn't really gone to the extremes about Jason I thought she would. And me being pregnant had seemed like a fun idea to her.

Something was up.

"If I wasn't thinking about you, I wouldn't have thought to call you, right?" Logic was an excellent weapon with my over emotional parent.

"Well, that makes sense. So, how is your new business? I told Pam all about it and she even pulled out her new phone and looked you up on the Google and everything."

"It's just Google."

"Right, the Google."

"No, Mom. It isn't *the* Google. It's just Google."

"Oh, well that's one more thing Pam doesn't know. I'll have to tell her we've been using the Just Google."

I closed my eyes and shook it off. I was just happy at this point she could use her remote controls without calling for help now.

"Anyway, we were looking at your website. It's very pretty. Pam seemed surprised but I told her you're *very* talented."

This was news to me. Maybe instead of calling my mom, I should check in with Pam occasionally.

"That's really nice, Mom. I'm glad you like it." And, as I said the words, I realized how true they were. I had never felt the direct approval of my mother before.

I stretched out in bed reveling in the moment, surprised how much it meant to me.

"So, what are you doing today that you're still in bed?" In the background, I heard the coffee grinder kick-in for her to-go cup that she brought with her to work.

"Oh, bad dream." Wasn't that the truth? "Had a rough time getting going today."

"I hate bad dreams. I used to have them all the time when you were little. I was always afraid I was going to do something that would get you hurt. I know it doesn't sound reasonable now, but every little thing worried me. I didn't want anything to happen to you."

"Really?"

"Yup. I knew I was all you had so the only thing that was worse than something happening to you was something happening to me."

Well, this was a morning of revelations.

"But," she prompted, "I don't think that's why you're calling me, is it?"

"Well, I'm not sure what you'll say to this. I'm almost afraid to mention it but..."

I paused, stalling out, afraid to go on. Suddenly, I wasn't sure I wanted someone picking Max apart. Especially someone who didn't know him. And, after all those nice things she just said, I kind of hated to ruin the conversation.

"You met someone." My mom said, a little laugh in her voice. "You met someone and listen to you panicking."

"Hey!" This isn't how this conversation was supposed to go.

"You didn't call Jayne because she'll tell you to just sleep with him, which, honey...I really hope Jayne isn't as promiscuous as she pretends to be. She's a nice girl under all that gruff. I'd hate to see something bad happen to her."

I held the phone away from my ear to make sure I'd really called my mother.

"Well...Yes. I kind of met someone. Maybe. I think."

"You don't know?"

Wasn't that the million dollar question?

"I mean, yes. I met someone. I met several someones. That girl Jenna's group of friends. They're very nice."

"Well, I'm glad to hear you've made some new girlfriends. But, like I said, if you really are pregnant and just not telling me, you can still come home. I told Bob he might have to help me paint the back room yellow."

Bob?

"First off, I'm really not pregnant. And secondly," I took in a deep breath, afraid I was not going to like the answer. "Who is Bob?"

"Oh, have I not told you about Bob?"

"Don't play innocent with me, missy. Who is Bob?"

"He's our new neighbor." That's my mom. I moved out almost a decade ago and she still calls him *our* neighbor. "He saw that a shutter was coming down so he fixed that and offered to take a look around at anything else I may have let slip."

"Well, that sounds very nice." And suspicious. "How old is this Bob guy?"

"Oh, I don't know. A couple years older than me at least. But he's very fit so it's hard to tell."

Mm-hmmm. Right.

"Mom, are you *dating* Bob?"

"Oh, no, honey. He's just a neighbor. He fixes stuff around the house and I make him dinner or something to thank him."

Great, my mother had a better social life than I did. Another reason I should be checking in with Pam. I was going to have to call my mom's best friend just to make sure the world was staying on its axis.

"So, he helps you out around the house and you cook him dinner." I considered my next question carefully. "And, do you pack him dinner or does he eat with you?"

"He eats here since it's easier. And just nice to have someone around." She sucked in a breath. "Kasey, what kind of interrogation is this?"

"I don't know, are you feeling interrogated?"

"I'm wondering why our new neighbor is so interesting to you."

I paused, considering my mother over the last few weeks and how less angry she'd been, how she'd not spent our conversations picking me or anyone else apart.

"Mom, are you happy?"

"What kind of question is that?"

"I just want to know you're happy."

"Kasey, I'll tell you this. I spent most of my life being afraid. I let that fear make me unhappy when there was no reason for it. Now, I'm making new friends and volunteering at the after school program and going to the gym. The only thing we really have to be afraid of is missing something. Everything else we can get over." She let out a little embarrassed sounding laugh. "I'm so sorry to ramble like that. I'm sure you didn't call to get a weird guru'y talk from me."

I closed my eyes and smiled. "You know what? Maybe that was exactly what I needed."

"Okay. Well, I love you, honey. Now, I'm off to Jazzercise with Pam."

I laid there wondering a few things. If my mom could stop being afraid, was the world ending? Could I trust Max? And...people still did Jazzercise?

But, most of all, could I trust myself to take a chance on Max?

TWENTY-SEVEN

A WESOME. I WAS hoping you'd be here!" Jenna dropped into the comfy chair next to me and propped her feet on the beat up coffee table in front of us. "I have an opportunity for you. You're going to be rich!"

That was a lot of excitement for this early. I wondered if Jenna actually saw exclamation points in her head when she spoke like that.

"What's up?" I set my mocha down in case all those exclamations led to arm waving.

"I was showing a girl in my writing group your mockups for my new branding stuff and she was all *ooooh* and *ahhhh* and the guy at the table next to us kept glancing over, and then he asked who did the work and I *raved* about you and he gave me his card and asked to meet with you this week."

"Wow. Seriously?"

"He loved it. He said from my obvious lack of website knowledge he'd assumed it would look like a standard theme just switched up for my color scheme, but that it was definitely personalized work. Just the kind of thing he was looking for." She gave herself a little high-five. "I played it cool and took his card and now you need to email him."

She held the smooth, cream card out to me, a huge smile on her face. I turned it over and read the front. John Simpson. Probably Opportunities, Owner.

Wow.

"I just have one question." Jenna dug her wallet out of her bag and stood. "What's a theme?"

I shook my head. The girl was a genius at what she did. I guess she could ignore everything else.

"It's a basic set up for a blog or site that people just stylize to fit what they want."

"So, it's like going into The Gap and asking them to give you the outfit on the mannequin?"

"Um, yeah." Why not? "Basically just like that."

"Got it." Jenna turned and bounced away to the counter while I stared at the card amazed at my first word-of-mouth sale. Amazed Jenna seemed to be my own personal fairy godmother. Everything was feeling so right.

I pulled up my new Lane Designs email account and shot John Simpson, Owner, a note right away with the preliminaries of what I was doing, attached links to other clients I'd done work for, and asked what questions I could answer for him.

Strike while the iron was hot. Plus, the only thing I really had to work on now was my own stuff since the wedding project for Mae was done. This was the perfect catalyst to get me moving.

I pulled out my to-do list and reordered it for a potential client. Pricing and finishing my own site bounced to the top right away. As in, do it now before your mocha cools, now.

Jenna settled back in across from me with her iced tea and flipped open her laptop.

"John said he'd want to meet with you in person to talk. He hates emails. He said something about a former partner, so I think he's a little gun shy. After the initial contact, he'll probably ask to meet you somewhere. He's a little awkward, phrases things funny. Like, he can't get his thoughts exactly out. He just kind of makes these half-statements and you have to fill in the rest while he figures out what he's trying to say. I swear half the conversation was me playing Guess the Next Word with him. He seems like one of those geniuses that can't focus on the day-to-day. But, I'm sure you're used to dealing with the Less Than Clear in your profession."

Unfortunately, that was true.

Jenna had been a dream client. She basically handed me her new covers with her publisher's write up and said, can you make my stuff feel like this.

"I'm sure I can make it work." I glanced at my email, waiting for the ding letting me know he'd emailed me back. I saw a long day of hitting refresh in front of me. "Thanks, Jenna. I really appreciate you doing this."

"Hey, what are friends for?"

I got to work on the final touches of my website and the brochure I'd need to print out if I was going to bring it with me to a face-to-face. One thing I did know about high ranking, eccentric clients: They wanted all the info and they wanted to be able to look at it over and over again.

I focused on getting it perfect. On getting it done. I focused on my pitch and my plan. I focused on what I could wear and how I would sell myself.

I focused on everything but Max Darby.

And that was probably for the best.

~~*~~

John had a dinner meeting downtown with out-of-town clients the next night but wanted to meet in the lounge beforehand to have a preliminary discussion.

The great news was I could write it off. The not so great news was I had to dress up.

I wandered through the hotel lobby and into the lounge, glad I'd still had a black sheath dress and little sweater for business meetings not packed away. I hadn't considered I'd still need to wear I'm A Grown-up Clothes now that I was typically working out of a café in yoga pants.

I did a sweep of the tables at the edge of the room before settling in at the bar to wait. I ordered a diet Coke and set my hand on the small tote bag next to me, comforted by all the materials I'd managed to pull together in two days for this meeting.

I pulled my little cardigan off and draped it over the bag. I was just discovering I was a nervous sweater—either that or this lounge had suddenly gotten really warm.

This was the beginning. He was my first real client. Jenna was my fairy godmother so she didn't count.

It wasn't long before a business man sauntered up to the bar and looked at me as if I might be who he was looking for.

"Hi. Are you looking for me?" I gave him my best smile, trying to make him like me right away. Starting off friendly would make turning me down or bartering with my prices harder. Or at least, that's what I hoped it would do.

"I certainly could be." He smiled back in such a familiar way that I knew we were going to get along just fine.

"I'm Kasey. Why don't you have a seat and we can chat a little."

"Great." John pulled out the high stool next to me and waved the bartender over. After ordering a drink he turned back to me, and took in my appearance right down to my shoes. I was really glad I hadn't shown up in jeans. "So, Kasey, how long have you been doing this?"

"I've just recently gone out on my own. It's definitely riskier, but you know what they say. Big risks, big wins."

He laughed, hopefully not noticing that the entire little speech was one hundred percent panic-driven bravado.

"Well, I like that. A woman who knows where she's going."

I smiled, because I certainly hoped that was true.

"I know this seems rude, but being new to this I thought we should discuss it right up front." With most people, I'd just send them a quote. The idea that I'd have to figure out how to deal with those who wanted to do everything in person was a bit overwhelming. "What are you looking for and how much are you looking to spend?"

"Wow, Kasey. That *is* direct. I like having things up front. There's no point in us getting to the point of no return and then not being on the same page."

"Exactly." Maybe this was going to be easier than I'd expected. "Obviously, the full package is going to be pricier. I mean, just the time involved in doing everything adds to the cost. But covering the basics a la carte can add up as well. I guess what it really comes down to is what's your pleasure?"

I smiled, trying to keep this professional but light.

John took a long sip of his drink, watching me over the rim of his glass.

I started to feel uncomfortable under the gaze, but assumed he was doing that thing Jenna talked about. That going-into-his-own-head-to-think thing.

"I mean," I continued, trying to pull him back to our conversation. "This is all about you and your needs."

"You're right. Of course. It's all about my needs." John set his drink down and leaned in. "I want the total package. Soup to nuts. I'm looking forward to seeing you in action."

Wow. Jenna must have really talked up my big corporate accounts history.

"Okay. Then, depending on any theme adjustments I need to make as we go, obviously I'll be making sure that you like everything I do. I won't get too far down any path without checking in. My goal is to have you completely happy with my work at the end of the day." I named an amount. I gave him a smile that hopefully was enticing. "Don't forget, I was trained by the best."

John straightened and ran his gaze over me again as if measuring me to see if I were worth that amount. I let him consider it. I knew what I could do. I'd shot up the corporate ladder because I was very good at what I did, and I knew when a man was trying to make me back down. If he was going to negotiate, that was fine. I'd built in a bit of a buffer, but I wasn't handing him a discount on a silver platter.

"That seems...excessive."

"You want the best, you have to pay for it. But, I can guarantee you won't regret it. I may just be branching out on my own, but I'm very good at what I do."

That seemed to give him pause.

"Kasey, are you sure you want to do this? It's hard enough being a working girl, but doing it on your own isn't always the safest route."

"That's very sweet." I reached out and patted his hand even though I knew it crossed the professional line. Or, maybe he just wanted to make sure I was going to be able to follow through. "But, if you're worried about my follow-through, there's no need. I'm ready to give you the best service available."

He smiled, a little tired, before pulling his wallet out to pay for his drink. Instead, he dropped a thick set of bills on the counter. I wasn't prepared for someone to give me his down payment in cash.

What if he wanted to pay all in cash? What if this business of his isn't on the up and up? I stared at the money a second before picking it up to hand it back to him.

"There's no need to give me this now. We can deal with that later."

"I'd rather be clear on what we're doing."

I still wasn't comfortable with this, but the worst thing that happened was I kept the cash in an envelop and gave it back to him if he didn't like my proposal.

"Okay. But, we'll have to arrange some type of guarantee for if this doesn't work out." I wasn't sure what a good protocol in this situation would be. "And obviously, you're going to want an invoice. It would be best all around if we handled this after the work was done. I'd like a deposit up front to ensure payment, but I'd rather not take cash."

John looked at me like this was an odd idea. He must really not be used to working with vendors. Maybe his new company was newer than I thought.

"So," he started as if not sure where this was going. Then, he pushed the money toward me again. "That's your payment, and you're going to give me the total package."

"Well," I tried to stall, trying to figure out how to get us back on track. "Let me show you my samples first. I want to make sure we can work together." I reached for my bag to pull out the shiny pamphlet I'd brought. "There's no reason to even talk about money before we do that."

"But, that's the amount?"

"Unless you add something on or change your mind, it's the amount I quoted."

"Okay. Kasey, I need you to stand up."

"Why?" Even for how odd Jenna had said he was, that seemed out there.

"Because I'm going to arrest you for solicitation and I don't want you to cause a scene if at all possible. We're just going to stand up and walk right out of here to where my partner is waiting."

"Solicitation? I wasn't soliciting. We had a pre-arranged meeting." As if I'd be going door-to-door at a high end hotel.

"Prostitution is illegal no matter how you find the John. Now, are we going to do this the nice way or are you going to risk embarrassing yourself, the patrons, and the establishment?" John stood, pushing his stool out of the way. "Let's just take this out the front door politely. I always add it into my report when the lady cooperates."

"But, I'm not a prostitute."

"Honey, you just agreed to give me the total package for an equally obscene amount of money."

"Total *marketing* package. I was meeting someone here to show him my web designs." I spun around to pull out my brochure, glad to finally get to show it to someone.

"Keep your hands where I can see them." John's voice went frigid. Gone was the charm and the smiles. It dawned on me he wasn't joking around.

This was not how I wanted to add to my recent cop run-ins. This was worse than any law-type thing I could think of. Including that little spring break run-in that shall not to be discussed.

"John, I'm serious. I was here for a business meeting."

"It's Officer Grant, and you can explain it to the booking agent downtown."

Downtown? Did people actually say that? Do we even have a downtown? I ran through all the neighborhoods I could think of but I don't think I'd ever heard anyone actually refer to a *downtown*.

He wrapped his oversized hand around my wrist, pulled me off the stool, and all thoughts of where we were going fled.

"Can I grab my sweater and bag?" After that *hands where I can see them* thing, I wasn't taking any chances.

"Grab it. You'll hand the bag to my partner outside. You can put the sweater on if you want." He looked at me, a little sadly like I'd disappointed him. "You shouldn't have gone off on your own. It's better to learn this lesson now."

Great. I was getting arrested for not being a prostitute, and he was lecturing me that I should have at least stayed with my pimp. I guess if I had a pimp at least I'd have someone to come bail me out.

TWENTY-EIGHT

I STARED AROUND the small, barred room trying to figure out where to go. You'd think with only a ten-by-ten area it wouldn't be too difficult of a decision. But, the far wall had two women leaning against it deep in a conversation I definitely didn't want to know about. Along each side of the holding cell were bunks. A girl stretched out on one, her pink thong clearly flashing the room of cops with her feet up like that. On the other, a woman in a bustier and a hot pink skirt sat examining her nails. I considered sitting at the other end, but there was a stain that...well, let's just say there was a stain and leave it at that.

I squeezed myself between the bed frame and the bars in the empty corner and hoped for the best.

The officer had told me he'd come back once my paperwork was processed and let me make my phone call. He'd kept asking me if I wanted a lawyer. I think *he* wanted me to have a lawyer. Where the heck was I going to get a lawyer, let alone how would I pay him?

But, who *would* I call?

I leaned my head against the bars, trying not to panic and wondering who to call. The only people I had in my phone were Jenna, Hailey, and people far, far away.

If I called Jenna or Hailey, they'd call Max. Of course, they would. If I were them, I'd call Max too.

But, then he'd be there, on the other side of this metal ringed room looking at me with that look, the one that said he was disappointed, annoyed, and exasperated with me.

But more, I pictured him giving up on me. All that chaos he said I created, the words he'd spoken to Jenna back before I'd known he wasn't someone to fear. Now he'd see them as true. He'd see me as that high maintenance, chaos creating, liability who would hold someone like him back. To a man who wanted to save, if not the world at least his corner of it, I'd be the train wreck running his life's work off the rails.

For the first time that night, I felt like crying. I felt stupid and short sighted and hopeless. How in the world could I compare a man who *demanded* to make dinner for me when I was hurt with that manipulative quasi-sociopath jackass I'd been tied to for years?

It figured that I'd wake up to what was right in front of me the moment I might lose it. I couldn't imagine how Max would feel about me being arrested. If I couldn't clear myself, I'd never find out. I'd never even put him on the spot. I'd never take the risk for my heart, and I'd never make him tell me that, no, he wouldn't date a girl like me.

I was now a girl like me.

If I could clear myself, I'd be lucky if he'd still speak to me.

Hopefully, there was a small chance I could get out of here without him knowing. Officer Grant had driven past the precinct closest to The Village. I could only hope that my mug shot wasn't being blasted to all the stations in town.

"Ooooh, sugar. It's shift change. All those cute young'uns will be coming in wearing those tight little blue pants."

The women behind me wandered over to the bars, setting themselves up in a line to watch the parade that was shift change. It was nice to know even ladies of the night couldn't resist a man in uniform.

If only I hadn't tried to for so long.

I tried to squeeze out of my corner, but no one was moving to let me by for fear of losing her space at the bars.

It was an odd, surreal power and role reversal that began the moment the first cop stepped through the door.

The ladies were right. This batch was young—all in their twenties. And their pants were definitely blue, some were even tight. But, each one reacted to the cat calls and whistles differently. Some ignored them, some blushed and turned away, some played it up. But none—not even the one who had probably never been able to run an eight minute mile— were left out. These women didn't prejudice based on race, looks, height, build…on anything.

"Oh, here comes one of my favorites. I'm telling you, I even got me that there Twitter to hear about him. Even just scraping past five-ten that boy's got some shoulders on him."

As soon as I heard the word *Twitter* I tried to leap over the crossbar of the bunk blocking me into the corner. There was no way with the week I was having there could be another local cop people followed on Twitter. It could only be—

"Tuesday?"

I took a deep sigh and turned back around to face Max striding across the room.

"Honey, you know Officer Max?" The larger girl with the neon fingernails looked me up and down like I'd just gained a bit of street cred.

"He tried to arrest me a few times last week." What else was I going to say? It was oddly true.

"Tuesday, what the hell are you doing in there?" Max wrapped his hand around the bar just above mine and glared at the women who'd all pushed closer so they wouldn't miss anything. "Ladies, I need a minute here."

"Ohhh, you don't have to tell me twice, Officer Hottie. I shoulda known you'd only be giving time to those lobby girls. Once you workin' out under the streetlights...pfft. No worries." They all followed Neon Nails lead and stepped back a whole foot.

Max kept glaring, but when he realized they weren't going anywhere—because, really, where the heck were they going to go—he turned back to me. "What the hell are you doing in there?"

"Ms. Lane is being charged with solicitation." The mean cop didn't even look my way.

"Honey, you gave them your real name. Don't you never give your real name. You picked a pretty little street name. Tuesday. I'm going to have to remember me that one."

I laid my head against the bars and closed my eyes. I guess I had a street name. That was something.

"Tue—Kasey, look at me. What's going on?"

There was no reason not to share. It wasn't like he didn't know I was in jail at this point.

"Jenna met this guy—"

"Jenna. Of course."

"He saw her showing a friend the new site I built for her with all the branding stuff and he was really impressed. So, Jenna got his email address and we'd arranged to meet in the lounge at the Plaza between his meetings and a dinner thing he had with some out-of-town clients. Just go over the basics. Only this guy walked up to me and when I asked if he was there for me, he sat right down."

"So, you asked him if his name was *John?*" At this point, Max's eyes were doing that twinkle thing that happened right before his super-powered-dimple came out.

Did I?

"If you laugh at me, Max Darby, you'll regret it. They have to let me out of here eventually."

"Right. So this John guy sits down and you ask him if he wants to get a room?"

"Darby, I'm processing this one." *John's* partner had taken over as soon as I'd gotten out of the lobby. He'd been nowhere near as nice and he was just getting worse. "I think I can ask the questions here."

Max just gave him a look and turned back to me. "So, then what happened?"

"Then he started asking for prices so I told him what I was charging for a total package and a la carte and I'd do whatever I could to please him."

"Exactly how much did you convince him you were worth?"

I gave him a number and Max glanced over his shoulder, giving the other cop a look that clearly said, *Seriously?*

"Hey. If I were for sale, I'm sure I'd be worth a lot. Maybe not like Beacon Hill Brownstone a lot, but at least a river view amount."

Max snorted at that point and I considered reaching my hands through the bars and wrapping them around his tanned, corded neck.

"What happened when you explained?"

"They wouldn't let me. I tried to show them my brochure, but every time I reached for my bag they just shouted, *keep your hands where I can see them*. And then they took my bag."

Max turned toward the mean, pushy cop, and I swear I saw him roll his eyes.

"Did you look in her bag and verify that she wasn't trying to sell you a website?"

"Did you make detective while I wasn't looking?"

"Nope. But I did get this special Boy Scout badge for common sense. I heard they only handed out two that year."

"Are you saying I made a bad arrest?" Now, the guy looked like he was going to go for Max's throat for me.

"I'm saying you're an idiot and if you don't get her out of that cell right now—"

"Don't make threats you'll regret."

"I won't regret it. You didn't let a confused, honest woman make an explanation. You probably walked her right into the charge without anything explicit." Max leaned in, like he was going to go after the other guy. "I'm really hoping you taped this collar, because her lawyer is going to *love* that. And then you throw her in a holding cell as if she was a criminal."

"I don't have lawyer," I whispered under their argument.

Max shot me a glare that was particularly hostile considering I'd become used to his typical scowls.

248

"She *is* a criminal."

"Let. Her. Out. *Now.*"

"You walk around here like you're the station's gift to the world. I'm reporting you to Internal Affairs. You can't walk in here and order me around. I think you're confused about the pecking order *Officer* Max. If you think I'm going—"

"Get her out or I will be the first person they call to the stand when she sues the city and you personally for wrongful arrest and detainment."

I reached through the bars and touched Max's shoulder trying to get his attention. Trying to calm him down.

Officer Vernane spun toward me, spitting as he shouted. "Get your freaking hands in the cell before I add accosting an officer to the charges."

I yanked my hand back through the bar, watching it shake in front of me. How had this gotten worse?

"Vernane. Darby. What is going on in my station?" An older man in a crumpled button down, the sleeves rolled to his elbows, stomped across the room, intent on the two men in front of me. "I have to hear you two are about to come to blows over a hooker while I'm meeting with the Mayor's assistant?"

"I'm not a hooker." No one looked my way.

"She's not a hooker." Max repeated.

"Darn it, sweetheart," Neon Nails chimed in. "I thought we were finally classing up the joint. Maybe you want to start working with us. Show us how you wrap a man like that around your pinky."

"Oooohhh, Sharlene. Look at her. You know what's wrapping Officer Max." The ladies laughed as Max turned bright red and I fought back more tears.

The boss guy looked toward us, then back at Max and the Detective.

"Vernane?"

"Markson picked her up in a lounge. She offered him services for money."

I watched Max's hands curl into tight fists at his sides, but he didn't move a muscle beyond that.

"Is this true miss?" The man looked at me, his gaze running over my outfit and the way I'd managed to shove myself in that tight corner where no one could get to me.

"Kind of."

"Kind of is not an answer I'd take on the stand."

"I was offering to build him a website. That's what my services are. I do corporate branding and just started running my own business. I was meeting with a man I'd only emailed with before."

I'd hoped just saying it all out loud would magically open the cell. No such luck.

"Darby?"

"Kasey is a friend. She's subletting my best friend's apartment. She builds websites. She's doing one for Jenna right now. Actually, it's Jenna who hooked her up with this John guy."

"Oh, Jenna." The boss guy's face softened into a smile. "How's our girl? I loved that kitten thing she did to you a few weeks ago. Some of those little sayings the kids post are a riot."

I watched Max struggle with not arguing.

"Um. Right." Max pulled it together before he could get derailed by the Hashtag Situation. "So Jenna sent her to this meeting and there was some miscommunication."

The boss guy looked at me, a little nicer now that pixie Jenna's name was being thrown around. Seriously. My fairy godmother.

Except for the fact that I was here because of her in the first place.

"How do we get from building websites to sex upstairs?"

That was an excellent question.

Everyone turned and looked at me as if I was the one who had planned to have sex upstairs.

"I don't know, sir. I was talking about website and branding packages and next thing I know the guy's trying to give me cash. I told him not to give me the money before we made a deal, but he wouldn't take it back. I told him he could give me a deposit, but was confused that he didn't want an invoice. Then he was telling me to walk out nice and calm and not make a scene. He was very polite about it, but he wouldn't let me show him my brochures."

The girls behind me snickered.

"You didn't take the money?" Max leaned forward, his gaze turning slowly as he pivoted toward Detective Vernane. "Is that right, jackass? She wouldn't take the money?"

"She said she'd take it upstairs."

"I did not!" I started to reach through the bars again to Max and stopped. "I said I'd take the money once we came to an agreement on our deal."

"She didn't deny the deal." Detective Markson was on his feet now.

"She didn't take the money. No money, no clear defined service, no action…*no arrest*. I'm sorry, I'm just a beat cop, but I vaguely remember in college that being called something like entrapment…or was it wrongful arrest?

251

There's just so many things going on here I'm confused about what the real issue is."

Max was leaning against the bars now, doing that cocky pose he did that typically was aimed at me and ticked me off. I let my hand curl around the bar he leaned against, skimming across his lower back and taking comfort from the heat radiating off him. He shifted, pressing against it. I felt his confidence seep into me and set my trust in it. Max was many things. One of those was a man I was beginning to set my complete trust in.

Outside my cell, the three men faced off. Max looking cocky, Detective Vernane looking like he was going to punch Max, the boss looking as if he wanted fire both of them and quit.

And they were the ones in charge of my future. I'd somehow managed to hand my fate over to a man—well, three men—again.

TWENTY—NINE

I WALKED OUT OF the station and down the front steps, trying to get my bearings on where I was and how I was supposed to get back to my new home. Beside me, Max stood, my tote over his shoulder, watching me.

I was pretty much done for the night—maybe the whole week. There was nothing more lowering than being arrested for something you didn't do. Especially prostitution. Why couldn't I have been arrested for corporate espionage or recklessly parachuting off a skyscraper or something cool?

"Okay. Well. Thanks. I really appreciate your help." I reached for my bag, desperately needing to make a quick escape. More embarrassed than I'd been in my entire life. I had no idea how I was going to face him after this. I couldn't even face him now. I could feel the heat climbing up my neck and hoped I didn't look splotchy under the horrible 1940's lights framing the station's doors.

"Where are you going?"

"Home."

Max just looked at me as if he'd expected something else, or something more. But, I wasn't sure what to say. I just knew I was completely freaked out and looking at him made me want to crawl into his arms and hide my face in his chest and hope he wouldn't brush me off him like dryer lint.

And, it was too late. I knew it was too late. He'd told Jenna he had no interest in dating someone like me, someone who could end up in jail at any minute.

And now, I'd put him on the spot. Max would never have left me in there. Who knows what they'd do to him now. The kitten posters everywhere would look like nothing when they were done with him if this turned into an Officer Darby is Dating a Hooker thing. Especially since the captain guy made it clear he missed #OfficerMax and had pointedly asked when Jenna would be doing another one.

Max just looked at me, waiting for who knows what, before shaking his head and handing me my belongings.

"You know what, Kasey? You're on your own."

Um…okay? What?

I just looked at him trying to figure out what that meant.

"I don't need this. I don't need to be responsible for someone I'm not even responsible for. You aren't my fiancée or girlfriend. You're just this girl who can't manage to stay out of trouble and the truth is, that's your problem."

I dropped my eyes shut trying to figure out what that even meant. I hadn't asked him for anything. I never did. When I got tossed in the slammer—words I never thought I'd say—I *hadn't* called Max. I hadn't wanted to tick him off or make him think I was only calling because of what he could do for me.

Maybe I was naive, but I thought someone would listen to me. I thought at some point the officer would realize he'd made a horrible mistake.

Also, I thought telling people I was in jail would be embarrassing, so skipping that step would have been A+.

"You know what?" I grabbed my bag, yanking it down his arm and practically dislocating it. "I didn't ask for your help. I've *never* asked for your help. I just want to do my own thing but Mr. I Know Best likes to jump in and *fix* things to exactly how they should be. You go do your own thing. Don't worry about me. No one thinks I'm your responsibility but you."

I stormed down the station's stairs, his voice stopping me before I reached the sidewalk. "You didn't call me!"

I spun around, not sure what I was going to say or how I was going to justify that, but no. I didn't call him.

"I didn't..." How was I going to explain this?

Max marched down the stairs, stopping so close I could feel the heat of him.

"You were *arrested* and were sitting in a freaking holding tank in my precinct and you didn't call me."

I looked up at him, the distance too close and said the only thing that came to mind. "I didn't know it was your precinct."

If he'd been angry before, that was nothing like the rage that washed over him then, drawing his brows down and pushing the red so far up his neck it looked like it was choking him.

"And, I mean, they hadn't let me make my call yet."

It was clear he didn't believe I was going to call him. Which was the truth so what could I say?

"Are you serious?" Max stepped back and turned, storming away before returning just as angry. "That's what mattered? That you didn't know if I worked there or not? You were in *jail*. You have a cop at your freaking beck and call and you just sit there wondering who to call."

"I didn't think you were at my beck and call." I seemed to keep picking the thing most likely to make him angrier, because he actually flung his arms wide when I said that.

"You didn't call anyone." His voice carried over the nearly empty parking lot and echoed back to us. "You just sat there, in jail, not using your call. You're a smart girl. You know you could have demanded it. Or just told them to call me. But no. Nope. You just sat there. Doing it Kasey's way. Not letting anyone in."

I glanced away, worn out just from looking at all the anger rolling off of him on top of the really cruddy evening I'd had. The angry beat of his work shoes pounding up the stairs and the door being slammed behind me.

THIRTY

I 'M NOT GOING TO LIE. I'm beginning to think you're an idiot." Jayne shushed me as the stilted GPS voice in the background told her to turn right.

"I know. I have no idea what happened. I was standing there thinking Max was a guy worth taking a chance on, and then there was all this yelling and storming off."

I heard the voice tell her she was point-two miles from her destination. I stood and watched for her little beater-box car roll down my street. She pulled past the line of high-end SUVs and waved at me as she looked for a spot to pull in. I trotted down the front steps and pulled the lawn chair I'd borrowed out of the space I'd been holding for her. Typically, I hated that person. But I wasn't sure how much stuff she'd brought with her, so I figured we'd need to be close knowing her over-packing habit.

As she pulled in, I glanced in the car and shuddered just a bit. Her habit was getting worse. Jayne threw the car in park and hopped out, rushing around to give me a hug.

"Hey, girl making even more horrible decisions than normal!" Typical Jayne greeting.

"Hey, girl who seemed to bring everything she owned. What's up with that?" I pulled her onto the sidewalk, always a little afraid the local drivers wouldn't stop for human bodies, even in my quaint little neighborhood.

"Yeah, so. Surprise!" She glanced at the car, its back seat stuffed to the point of full. "I'm moving here!"

"Best news ever!" I flung my arms around her, pretty sure my life just got better by four. "You're moving here. This is nuts. You can't just move here. How are you moving here?"

"Well, I thought about what you said about starting your own business and all the work you were doing and how you were meeting people here and thought, I don't want to miss out on all that."

"You don't have to *move* here to be part of my life." That seemed extreme even to me.

"No. I know. But," She leaned against the hood, staring off down my over-manicured street. "You aren't the only one who could use a clean start."

There was more going on here than a visit, that was obvious.

"Why don't we throw your stuff—*some* of your stuff—upstairs and get a drink?" We were obviously going to have to do some heavy-duty planning for both of us.

"Can we go to the Brew Ha Ha?"

"You want to go to The Brew? Not a pub or something?" It seemed out of character for her to not want to try a local craft brew.

"You talk about it all the time and maybe I'll get to lay eyes on this hottie cop of yours."

"He's not mine. But, sure, we can go to The Brew."

We carried her bags upstairs and she ooh'd and aah'd over how cute the apartment was. We put her clothes in the small closet in the living room and headed on over to The Brew.

Of course, Abby was working. I was beginning to wonder when she wasn't working.

"Who's this?"

"Hi, Abby. I'm fine thanks. How are you?" I'd learned to just respond to her as if she'd said exactly what a normal person would.

"Right. Fine. Whatever. Who is she?" She pointed a suspicious glare at Jayne.

"This is Jayne. My best friend from home."

This didn't seem to win Jayne any points.

"So, she's here to visit?"

"Does it matter?" Jayne glared back at Abby.

Well, this was going to be interesting.

"Yes. John says I have to be nice to the regulars, so if you're going to be coming in all the time with this crew, then I have to be polite."

"Just to be clear, you'll only be polite to me if I'm going to be a regular?" Jayne glanced my way and I tried to tell her with a strong look not to engage.

"Right."

"So, yes. I'm going to be a regular."

Now Abby had good reason to look suspicious. "Are you just saying that so I'm polite to you?"

"Is this your version of polite? Because, I have to tell you, it kind of sucks. I almost want to say I'm *not* going to be a regular to see how you treat normal people."

"Jayne, for the love of stars, do *not* tempt fate!" This was the scariest thing that had happened in days. And I'd just gotten out of jail.

Jayne and Abby stared each other down, their gazes clashing over the counter. It was a match of wills for the centuries.

"Abby! Stop glaring at the customers." John's voice came from the back room. There were days he didn't even bother to come out to correct her any more. Just shouted from where he was. I considered buying him one of those zappy collars people trained their dogs with.

That was probably illegal, though, and I was done dancing on the dark side.

"She can't decide if she's a regular or not," Abby shouted back without bothering to look away from Jayne. "You said I had to be nice to the regulars."

I could hear the long suffering sigh from the backroom, before a chair-scraping sound and John's tread pacing to the front of the café.

"I said don't be rude to the regulars. Not you *only* had to be nice to the regulars."

"But you didn't say I had to be nice to anyone or not to be mean to the drop-ins."

John's gaze narrowed on Abby and for the first time I saw a spark of anger in it. Abby must have seen it too, because she turned toward him, her hands clasped at her waist.

"You want to learn to run a restaurant? To be a manager? Or do you want to be a petulant child no one wants to work with?"

I sucked in a breath and glanced toward Jayne who was looking at this as if it were all interesting. She could have no idea how much John and the customers put up with from Abby. It was almost a rite of passage to have to deal with her. But, there was direct and then there was the over-the-top rude.

That must be the line.

"I'm not..." Abby glanced at us, a quick burst of panic crossing her face. "I'm not..."

I wished Jenna was here. Abby speechless was a new thing.

"It's fine." Jayne leaned over the counter so John could see her past the pastry display. "I provoked her. She wasn't being rude, just specific."

John glanced between them, his expression softening. "Right. Okay. Remember, rude is bad. Direct is...well, we'll work on that."

Without even waiting to be introduced, John went back to whatever he was doing in the backroom.

"Sorry." Abby was looking at Jayne as if she were a super hero. "I'm...*direct*. And John is a bit stressed right now."

I glanced around the very quiet Brew and hoped that the death knell of my new favorite place wasn't being sounded.

I headed over to our overstuffed chairs and settled in, waiting while Jayne chatted with Abby as she finished our drinks. The Brew couldn't be in trouble. I wouldn't let it. I'd use my super-marketing powers to help if that were the case. A quick conversation with John was in order, but definitely not today. Maybe some evening events.

The Brew After Dark. That could be fun.

And profitable.

Jayne headed over and plopped down in the seat beside me, looking content and rested for someone who'd just driven over ten hours.

"So, this is the place." She glanced around. "Interesting. More active than I expected."

"But not active enough from what Abby says. I'm going to talk to John about some marketing. He's the one who helped me find a place to live. We'll call it even. Not that I don't love having The Brew to myself, but no customers equals no Brew."

"Great. So that gives us one more job, even if it is pro bono."

I could feel myself freeze, the cup halfway to my lips as I asked, "Us?"

THIRTY—ONE

"YES." JAYNE SET HER mug down and turned to face me, her game face on already. "Us. As in you and me. As in, I'm going to be your assistant."

"Except, I'm not hiring."

"Yes you are."

"No. I'd know if I were hiring. And I may have just lost my big job because of a little problem with getting arrested instead." Which was still eating at the back of my mind. I had no idea if at this point if I had a record or not. Max could have gone back in and said, *Forget it. Charge her.* There could be a warrant for my arrest right now. I could be a fugitive. I'd have to go on the run and never contact my friends or mother again...which, with how odd she'd been on the phone this week, might not be the worst news ever anyway.

Jayne snapped her fingers in front of my face. "Where'd you go?"

"Mexico." That's where fugitives went, right? I had to head for the border.

"Mexico? Really?" Jayne gave me a more skeptical look than usual. Which, I'm not gonna lie, was pretty hard.

"No. Not *really*-really. I was just wondering if I was a fugitive from justice."

"Justice, no. Poor decision making, absolutely." Jayne took a deep sip of whatever Abby gave her as a peace offering and smiled. "But, as your new admin, I'm here to make sure that only good decisions are made from now on."

"Jayne, for real, I can't afford an admin. I don't know what you're thinking. I can't even afford to cover my rent. I'm living on my severance and if things don't pick up before the end of that, my savings. I can't pay you."

Jayne slammed her mug down, catching even Abby's attention. "Did you hear me ask to be paid? Did you hear me say I was going to do XYZ for ABC?"

"That's how jobs work."

"Listen up, Sparky McLawbreaker. This is how friendships work. You need help. I'm help. You suck it up and take the help." She leaned forward into my space, her voice dropping so no one beyond the couches would have heard us if John had more than the two of us there. "You are going to learn that not everyone is your emotional manipulative ass of an ex-boyfriend. You are going to learn that some of us actually care for you. Kasey. Kasey the person. Not, Kasey who can do something for us. And..." She pointed a finger at me, stabbing it through the air in a way that looked potentially deadly. "And you are going to like it."

Everything I could think of to respond with started with *But*...I had a sneaking suspicion anything that started that way would get my butt kicked.

"Listen, Kasey, I get it. You've never really had someone who was there for you through it all. Someone *for* you." She waved her hand when I tried to jump in, tried to say she had been. "No. Not me either. If I had, I wouldn't have been afraid to rock the boat about how Jason treated you and talked to you. But, I'm here now and we might as well do this friend thing right from here on out."

"You don't owe me because of the Jason stuff."

"I know. Well, maybe a little. But that's not what I'm thinking." She leaned back into her chair, picking her drink back up and apparently switching out of attack mode. She slid me a sly look. "Well, maybe you've had one person who hasn't let you down."

I knew what she was saying, knew it was true. But, danced the dance anyway, afraid to say his name out loud as if it were to admit something horrible had been taken from me that had never truly been mine to begin with. "Jenna?"

"Don't be dense."

Right. I'd been dense too long. I nodded, still afraid to say it.

"Okay, so," Jayne slipped back into business mode that easily, dragging me with her. "Here's the deal. I need to focus more on my art. You need to focus more on the creative end of your business. I need someone to create a site and brand to sell me that's so kickass people don't even notice how quasi-talented I am. You need to stop wasting time tracking mailing lists. Also, someone who creates original art for you wouldn't hurt. Together, we can take over the world."

Okay, when put like that it didn't sound so bad.

"But," she raised a hand as I started to drift into planning mode. "You first. It's a favor. It's me having your back. It's you learning to trust people to not let you down or take over. I mean, I could *totally* take over and make your business whatever I want it to be while you're off being creative. But I'm your friend, *sooo…* "

I felt the churn of panic deep in my gut. Could I hand over a significant part of my business structure to someone I hadn't really talked to in a year? Could I believe that she had my best interests at heart and wasn't just looking to see what she could get from this?

I took a deep breath, realizing I was going to have to either plunge in or isolate myself from Jayne for good. She'd pushed me out on a limb and I had no idea how thick it was. Would it hold?

I glanced at Jayne and thought, *Yeah. It'll hold.*

Or she'll catch me.

THIRTY–TWO

I DREAMT OF MAX…of course I did. But, this time, not kittens. Just Max standing on the far side of the road dressed in everyday clothes looking at me as if I'd betrayed him.

He glanced down the street, both ways, but every time he went to step out into the road, a car raced by, forcing him back onto the sidewalk.

Okay, subconscious. I got it.

~~*~~

"So, this is great." Jayne smiled at me over the counter as I spooned her out an omelet. "You, me, a condo built for one extremely small person with very few belongings."

I laughed. Jayne had been there two nights and was already ready to move on. I knew she wouldn't last much longer when she'd had to go to her car four times to get dressed this morning.

"You're saying that the free rent of a couch in the most beautiful part of town is too expensive?"

"I'm saying, I need a closet that's bigger than a dumbwaiter. Since you don't have that for me to commandeer this is going to have to come to an end sooner rather than later. But"—she grinned over her mug as she pulled up Craigslist on her laptop—"we'll always have The Village."

And, let's be honest. The Village was as close to Paris as either of us was going to get in the next few years.

"Right, so I'm going to look at some places today." She noted a couple things on her phone while I scrubbed the skillet, trying not to panic again.

I was, perhaps, the most emotional-swingy person I knew lately. Leave me alone! Don't leave me!

"Today?" I focused on a tiny spot of burnt egg, attacking it with my nearly worn out sponge. "But you just got here."

"Right, but it's the middle of the month. If I want to find something for next month, I have to find it now."

"So, you'll be here a few weeks then, huh?" Yeah, subtle Kasey.

Jayne glanced up, her gaze narrowing. "I'm not deserting you."

"Right. I know."

"I'm not taking over and I'm not deserting you."

"Uh-huh."

"Dude, you're nuts. You know that right?"

Oh yeah, I totally knew that.

"So, where do you think you'll move?"

Jayne shut the laptop down, and gave me her full attention. "I don't know. Somewhere in town. Hopefully on the transit line by The Brew. Maybe the other side of The Brew, but there's no way I'll find another deal like this in The Village."

I nodded, it was unfortunately true. But… "We should ask John. He knows everything. And if there's not, maybe Abby can scare someone out of house and home for you to sublet."

"Right. Because I want to be beholden to Abby. That sounds safe." Jayne shoved more of her omelet in her mouth before going on. "But, I'm going to need to rely on you to help me. I want something clean, safe, and not filled with college students, in a place that I can afford."

Finally. Something I could do for someone else. We got out the transit neighborhood map and started marking off areas she should look. After a few calls, she had an appointment to meet with a girl who needed to let a room in her apartment.

"It's too bad you didn't get here a month ago. We could have lived together." I closed my eyes and pictured myself borrowing her artist cliché clothing. Then shook that off when I looked like a little kid playing dress up in my head.

"Yeah, except for that guy you were moving in with and all that."

"Oh. Yeah. I totally forgot about him."

We laughed, knowing that forgetting a guy was as easy as not thinking about him for a few hours at a time until hours were days and days were months and months were, *Oh, guess who I ran into the other day.*

Jayne being Jayne was going to go alone. I think she was afraid I'd flip out on the girl and question her about her entire life. Which was probably true, so I didn't fight her too hard.

I settled in for a day of making lists of everything that needed to be done for my business and every idea I could think of for Jayne's marketing.

But mostly, I stared at the page and thought of Max.

THIRTY-THREE

T HE KNOCK AT MY door surprised me as I sat shoving Ben & Jerry's down my throat, not even bothering to taste it, just hoping for the emotional fulfillment it was supposed to bring.

I glanced around for a napkin but gave up and wiped my hand across my mouth. Not that it mattered. I was pretty much a mess anyway. I'd gotten chocolate syrup on my shirt when I'd given up trying to open the top and had sawed through the plastic nozzle with a bread knife.

Don't judge me.

I patted my hair with my cleaner hand, hoping I'd managed to get the knots to at least lay smooth, and then opened the door.

"You're supposed to ask who it is." Max stood there, looking tired and rumpled and annoyed again.

"It didn't seem to matter."

"Damn it, Tuesday. Of course it matters." He took my arm, pulling me back into the apartment and slamming the door behind us. "You think I don't worry about this crap? You want me to let you just skip along through life opening doors to strangers and letting men think you're a hooker?"

"Um, no?"

Even though I was ninety-nine percent sure that was the right answer, he still glared at me.

"I don't want to be the boss of you. I don't want to be the guy telling you how to live your life. I get that you're a capable grown woman. I'm not looking to babysit someone. No grown man is. We're looking for an equal, someone to take care of when she *needs* us to. And someone who takes care of us when we need it. Courtesy is not the same thing as controlling."

He slammed his keys down on the counter and paced back and forth looking utterly capable and more masculine than any man had a right to. It wasn't even the uniform and gun. It was just Max.

"I don't want this." He waved a hand around in what seemed to include my apartment, me, and anything within four hundred feet of him. "I don't want this chaos, but damn it all if I don't want you."

I'd begun to hope when he'd shown up angry. That shriveled and died as he stormed around the little space. "You don't want me?"

"No," he said, and my heart dropped. "No, that's the *problem*. I do want you. I wanted you when you were sitting there reading that paper upside down after attacking your ex's car. And climbing in a window backward in your underwear. And maiming trees. And lying about what you liked because you didn't know. And being sweet to Jenna and giving the gym a try because Hailey wanted you to. I liked you arguing with me at game night and smiling at me over dinner. And that is exactly the problem."

"The problem is that you like me?"

He stopped pacing and ran his hand over the short cropped hair at the back of his neck. "Yes."

I felt the anger building up in me, rising over the bad night and the absurd almost-arrest and everything else.

"*You're* mad because you're interested in *me?*"

"Yes."

"Really?"

"Yes…" he sounded less sure this time.

"I was ready to just be on my own. To find my own way. I didn't do anything except try to keep my distance from you. But, no!" I tried to use my inside voice, but I was already way past that. I blame being drunk on ice cream. "No! You had to be all Mr. Charming. Mr. Let's Go to a French Film and let me make you dinner and how about going dancing and have you seen the X-men and let me rescue you from prison. I'm trying, here! I'm trying! And the harder I tried to stay away from you, the more you chased me. So, no! No you don't get to be mad and lecture guy now. You don't get to tell me you're walking away and just leaving me standing here after knocking down every wall I have."

Max paced away and came back at me so fast I backed up into the counter behind me until he was barely a breath away.

His voice dropped, pulling me even closer. "Every wall?"

I nodded.

"Every wall has to mean just that, Kasey. I don't have it in me to keep trying to break through to you."

I nodded again, afraid anything I might say would be the wrong thing, the thing that would ramp this all back up again.

I'd just put my heart way—*way*—out there and was desperately afraid.

Max's hand slid around my waist and pulled me the last distance between us. "No going back. This is your last chance."

As he looked down at me I realized he was right, this was my last chance. So, instead of letting him change his mind, I went up on my toes and kissed him.

He went still, the muscles in his arms tightening where I hung on to him, as if at any moment he'd shove me away and make a sprint for the door.

And then, as I was starting to fear I'd read that wrong, that somehow all his talk had meant my last chance to get my act together, not to get my man, his arms came around me, banding me to him. His mouth took over the tentative kiss I'd begun and nearly annihilated me in the heat of him.

Years with Jason hadn't felt like this. *Nothing* had ever felt like this. Max was, and probably would always be, a man who needed to be in control. But, let's just say that when it came to kissing Max, I wouldn't have it any other way.

THIRTY-FOUR

TUESDAY, I'M COMING to get you for breakfast. You're going to wait in your apartment and ask me who I am when I knock on the door. Then you're going to hold my hand as we walk to The Brew where I'll buy you a muffin."

The same heat I'd felt the night before when I'd walked Max to the door to say goodnight and instead he'd pushed me against the door and kissed me everythingless again, rushed over me.

"Okay," I breathed, feeling ridiculous and attempting not to giggle.

"I'm serious."

"I know."

I got it now. I got that Max needed to do things he thought the guy should do. Stupid little things that, yes, I could do on my own. But, it made him absurdly happy to walk me to my door. It didn't mean he didn't think I could find my way home on my own.

"Okay, then." He sounded disappointed as if he'd expected a fight. "I'll see you in ten."

"I'll meet you downstairs if you're late," I challenged, just to keep him on his toes.

"That's my girl."

The phone went dead before I could figure out if I liked that or not.

Which was probably for the best because I really, *really* liked it—not that I'd ever admit that to him.

I sat in my window like an idiot watching him walk down the street, looking both ways twice before crossing the nearly dead street. Exactly nine minutes later, Max knocked on my door.

I opened it.

"Tuesday." The exasperation was clear. I'd gotten to know him so well, that I could even read this specific formerly-inscrutable look.

"I knew it was you." I grinned and let him deal with that. Grabbing a sweater and my keys, I locked the door and headed down the stairs, expecting him to follow.

On the sidewalk, I waited as he jogged down the last few steps and turned toward The Brew, stopping when he realized I wasn't with him.

"What?"

"You promised there'd be hand-holding."

Max shook his head before wrapping my hand in his big mitt. "Right. Hand-holding. Look out. I'll be opening the door on the other end."

"Okay."

We walked to The Brew discussing what we were going to tell everyone about my stint in the slammer.

"And?" Max gave my hand a squeeze as he asked it.

"And, what?"

"And, what are we going to tell them about this?" He waved a hand between us.

"I was going to tell them that you blackmailed me into dating you to get me out of jail." I gave him my sauciest grin. "Why, what were you going to tell them?"

"That you promised to rub my feet every day for a month if I'd pretend to be your boyfriend."

My heart skipped a beat at the word *boyfriend*, panicking a bit more than I'd expected.

"Breathe, Tuesday. It's just a status, not a prison sentence."

"Right. Sorry." I snuck a look at Max trying not to look hurt. "No. Really. I'm sorry. I've tossed my whole plan away and it takes some getting used to. But, this is…good. This is really good."

"Whatever you say."

Because that was probably the only time I'd ever hear him say that, I just smiled and soaked it in. And planned to spend the next lifetime dreaming of kittens.

~~*~~

Want More Brew?
THE BREW HA HA SERIES

It's in His Kiss
The Last Single Girl
Worth The Fall
The Catching Kind

BREW AFTER DARK Shorts
Love in Tune
Sweet as Cake

~*~

YA Books by Bria Quinlan

Secret Girlfriend (RVHS #1)
Secret Life (RVHS #2)
Wreckless

~~*~~

Bria Quinlan writes sweet and sassy rom coms because if you can't laugh in love…when can you? Check out her non-story ramblings www.briaquinlan.com.

~~*~~

Thanks so much for reading *Worth the Fall*. It was a fun story to write because I'd long ago promised my best guy friend (known to everyone on Twitter as Wine Guy) that I'd stop tweeting about him if people stopped asking about him. They never did. This past year, he took off several months from work to move his mama to the US to be with him as she died. He was incredibly moved by all the tweeps who sent him prayers, good thoughts, and wanted updates on Mama Wine Guy. He's a technical manual reader, so rom coms aren't his thing, but he loved that he and the twitter world I dragged him into got a shout out here with #OfficerMax.